SALVAMAR
A TALE OF SALVAGE & DEEP DIVING

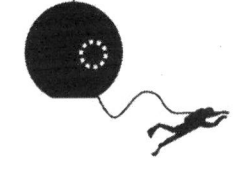

DOMINIC L. MILLER

CONTENTS

Acknowledgements
01. *Highroller* 1
02. Sink or Swim 9
03. Borneo Beckons 17
04. Aquanaut 26
05. Bell 35
06. Maserati 43
07. Newhaven 51
08. The *Dalhousie* 60
09. Finger Trouble 66
10. Rhône 76
11. Cabo Frio 84
12. Helicopter 93
13. East Indiaman 102
14. Back to Brazil 109
15. Way out 117
16. Research 125
17. Announcement 133
18. Decompression 139
19. Report 147
20. Comando Vermelho 158
21. Feeling Effects 165
22. *Titanic* 178
23. Making Tracks 185
24. Définitif Plongée 192
Author's Note

Copyright

© 2019 by Dominic L Miller

All rights reserved. No part of this book may be reproduced or used in any manner without the express written permission of the publisher except for the use of brief quotations in a book review. Sorry, has to be said ☺

ISBN: 9781696212458
Imprint: Independently published

Edited by Hugh Barker
Cover art and design © by Dominic Forbes

Based On True Events

Having said that...

All characters featuring in this work are fictitious. Any resemblance to real persons, dead or alive, is purely coincidental. Maybe.

IN MEMORY OF BRIAN WORLEY

LOG BOOK 591

Instructions

1. Identification of the person to whom this Log Book refers should be by photograph in the appropriate place, which is to be overstamped by the issuing company. The diver's signature is also required in the space provided.

2. Medical examination to the requirements of the appropriate authority must be carried out by a registered medical practitioner. Such examinations must be continuously updated in accordance with the regulations in force.

3. During diving operations all log books are to be completed and signed daily by the diving supervisor. Countersigning of divers' log books must be carried out by company management either at three-monthly intervals or on termination of employment.

4. Log books must be available and produced on demand to Inspectors having authority.

QUALIFIED TO UNITED KINGDOM

DIVING STANDARDS.

Association of Offshore Diving Contractors

PROFESSIONAL
DIVER'S LOG BOOK
Person to whom this log book relates

Name: BRIAN WORLEY Date of Birth: ...37

Address: 116, EASTWOOD ROAD
RAYLEIGH — ESSEX. TEL

Change of Address: ....

Change of Address: ....

Change of Address: ....

Signature: [signature]

Acknowledgements

Writing Salvamar would not have been feasible without the considerable input of the following people.

Oliver De Kermel, Malcolm Ferguson, Carol Clarke, Kathleen Guinot, Pat & Bill Hicks, David Miller, Neil Hicks, Julie Ebbs, Tom Wingen.

And it would certainly not have been possible or anywhere near as interesting without the constant assistance, support and guidance from the following good people (in no particular order):

Anne & Georges Arnoux, Colleen Miller, Terry Worley and Frank & Dee Lee.

A special word must be reserved for Lina Adam, the beautiful lady who has tolerated my daydreaming and fevered note-taking for the last year. Not forgetting the time needed to actually write the story too. All the daydreaming and sneaking out of bed before sunrise will be less frequent from now on.

Salvamar was written over the previous six months in the following places; Haarlem in the Netherlands, Cologne in Germany, Cockfield and Chertsey in the UK, Pula and Medveja in Croatia and Arles in France. This serves as proof I get around just as much as my uncle did. It was a huge challenge from the outset to fit everything in. But I have loved every single second of learning more about my uncle than he, or I, ever thought possible. And now it's your turn.

Thank you all. Dominic

September-2019

SALVAMAR – A TALE OF SALVAGE & DEEP DIVING

01. *Highroller*

"It's a bit rough, innit Bri?" asked Bill, in his continually amused way.

A warm onshore breeze had picked up overnight, agitating the Mediterranean Sea into an angry team of white-capped horses. The cool spray created just above the surface swirled and shifted with a rainbow sheen. Occasional hot gusts carried the briny mist inland. Languid waves slapped against the end of the pitted concrete breakwater at the mouth of the harbour. Flags throughout the harbour were pulled taut by the wind, indicating its direction. The Rock of Gibraltar dominated the skyline across the bay to the east, a gathering of flat clouds snagged around the summit. Container ships along the coast had dropped anchor and were stationary: the harbour pilots were unable to reach them to steer them into port. Some opportunistic seagulls cawed above Brian and Bill, hoping for some tasty bait scraps from what they saw as two more fishermen.

Brian, with his overlong ebony hair held in check by a saliva-lined face mask just above his forehead, looked out at the sea and couldn't disagree. His ink-black colouring was out of step with his siblings: it was often blamed on a dormant Portuguese branch of the family. His father had often made the accusatory observation that Brian "had the touch of the tar brush" about him. Another sage observation his father made of his second and youngest son was on the subject of his career. "You know your problem son, don't you? You're smarter than your bosses but you don't want to be like them!"

Over his broad, bronze shoulders hung a freshly filled scuba tank and an unzipped wetsuit top. Beneath that was a pair of wide-sided black swimming trunks. A moustache curved around the corners of his mouth, the lower portion of his jaw distended whenever he was nervous or thinking. On that morning, he felt a little of both, but he had to retrieve his boat, *Highroller* regardless; it had been impounded by Spanish Customs officers from non-payment of import taxes. It was a 32-foot pleasure cruiser, very much out of its comfort zone of cruising inland waterways or staying safely moored in Marseille or Nice. That morning he was planning on taking *Highroller* for a quick blast across the choppy waters of the bay, from Algeciras into the welcoming arms of British waters of Gibraltar, beyond the reach of Spanish custom officers.

"Yeah, it's magic. They won't chase us in this wind," Brian replied: the wind blowing onshore from the Med made Brian hard to hear, especially as he had the regulator held in the side of his mouth.

Bill was a kindly soul; a breezy father of two and fellow larrikin. Although employed back in Essex as a Health & Safety officer at a petrochemicals plant, he frequently rode his moped the six miles to work wearing a full face mask of the Incredible Hulk beneath his helmet. Dressed in ivory swimming trunks and t-shirt, Bill had joined Brian for a small swim on the boat, or that is what Brian had told him. He was always welcome aboard after all the help he had lent Brian in fixing *Highroller* up back in Newhaven, before relocation to the Mediterranean.

Now he realised Brian was planning on going for a slightly longer kind of swim.

"Brian, you're bloody doo-lally!"

"Just be ready to swim out to me, but I'll get as close as I can."

"Jesus Christ Bri. What about the Maserati?"

"Oh yeah," Brian laughed. "Could you drive round to Gibraltar for me? Meet me there instead?"

"Christ. OK!" This wasn't a refusal by Bill to participate: as such it technically marked the moment at which he became an accessory. Brian just smiled as he pulled his mask down over his face and pushed the regulator into his mouth. After looking up into the sun a final time, he pulled his thumb and forefinger together to make a circular 'OK' signal before jumping flippers first into another world, one that made more sense to Brian. When it came to any uninitiated observers above the water, they could have been forgiven for thinking they had just witnessed a James Bond screen test by Burt Reynolds: the scene was only missing a harpoon gun.

Life was always simpler underwater. Under the sea Brian could pull a curtain across the world. For all the commotion above the waves, it was always the same beneath them; cool, serene and weightless. Life was complex above the waterline, but was more straightforward below. The hot sun was tempered by the cool turquoise water, although Brian was also used to much colder conditions. With the wind noise muted, only his breathing was audible as he pulled himself deeper into the harbour from one anchor chain to another, always looking up for the 'X' he had painted on the underside of *Highroller*, when she had last been in dry dock.

Just before starting the Maserati, which was parked by the start of the breakwater Brian had just leapt off, and burning his back on the scalding leather seats, Bill shook his head and repeated his assumption to himself, "Brian, you ARE doo-lally!"

Through the numerous moorings Brian found the crude 'X' marked on the hull of *Highroller*. As he waited just below the surface to check for any evident movement between the boat and the quayside, he slowly drew his knife through the bowline that was drooping down into the water. With eyes barely above the surface like a frog, he slipped off his air tank and mask, letting them drop below him, as they had served their purpose. Slowly transferring his weight aboard, he climbed onto the shallow marlin-board at the stern of *Highroller* and cast off the rope tethering the rear to the harbour. The door panel on the enclosed awning was cautiously unzipped enough for Brian to slide through, keeping as low to the floor as possible while he moved. As he shifted he was continually blowing water out of his mouth as it drained down from his dripping, saturated hair.

Captain Worley, as he dubbed himself since buying *Highroller*, reached for his sunglasses stored in a cubby besides the metal steering wheel and unzipped his wetsuit halfway to reach inside for the keys. He took one last look behind him before firing the engines and gently pushing both throttle levers and casting away as silently as he had surfaced just seconds earlier. Brian spun the wheel in the direction of the harbour mouth, anticipating an agonizing journey across the relative calm of the harbour before his ride across the white horses in the bay. He could see that Bill was already on his way around to Gibraltar as the Maserati had moved from the beginning of the causeway.

Trying not to draw unwanted attention, Brian maintained a semblance of calm and normality before dropping the throttle levers flat on the dashboard once he had reached the end of the breakwater. The two inboard engines roared and chewed the wake to an angry, fizzing foam. The bow lifted while the rest of the hull slammed violently against the water, jumping from wave to wave. The engine note rose every time the propeller was momentarily out of the water. Then the sirens and announcements started, revealing that customs officers had noted *Highroller* leaving their custody and were already on Brian's tail. It wasn't too rough for them to pursue after all. However, if conditions had been calmer, Brian wouldn't have stood a chance. But he did have a chance in these conditions.

"Regreso al puerto. Estas bajo arresto. Esto no es una advertencia. Abriremos fuego en 30 segundos. Regreso al puerto de inmediato."

Their threats were not a bluff, but Brian had no clue what they were saying so he ploughed on regardless. Warning shots were then fired above *Highroller* and Brian heard them hiss past. Then the aim dropped to the water around the boat. The shots came in bursts of sporadic fire, each creating a small explosion as it broke the surface to his right and left. But he endured. Slamming and bobbing and roaring across the Bay of Gibraltar. Brian held his right hand flat on the throttle levers, continually tightening his grip on the steering wheel. There was no going back now. He needed *Highroller* back.

"Regreso al puerto. Estas bajo arresto. Esto no es una advertencia. Ahora estamos apuntando a su embarcación y abriremos fuego en trece segundos. Regrese a puerto inmediatamente."

"Come on, you *baastard!*" Brian repeated, over and over, as the boat crashed against the waves. He preferred the northern English vernacular as he felt it gave cursing more emphasis. "Hold together, you *baastard!*"

He used the stationary vessels as best he could to shield himself from the gunfire, winding a course through the anchored obstacles. He had to stand over the wheel, with his legs braced wide and absorbing the larger impacts. In the cupboards around the living area, glasses were smashing and plates were cracking. Halfway across the bay he realised that the two customs boats were gaining. The gunfire was getting louder and the splashes from the bullets larger: but he just kept his course for the left of the Rock. His sense of direction wasn't one of his strengths, but the Rock was as good a landmark as he could have hoped for, as the shoreline was hidden when he was in the trough of one of the deep waves. The view was further obscured by the layers of encrusted salt on the glass, laid down during its confinement by the Spanish. It was much like navigating with cataracts. If *Highroller* made it, there would be more repairs Brian and Bill would be needing to make. His constant shift of view, from front to behind, further disorientating the Captain.

"Just a bit further, you *baastard!*" Brian repeated, more in hope than certainty. No matter how big the jump or how damaging the landing was, he just kept his right hand pressing down hard on that throttle.

The customs officers were within a boat's length of *Highroller*, circling menacingly across the wake with a clear shot of the frantic skipper when they were forced to abort the chase, as they didn't want to cause a diplomatic incident with their British neighbour. Once he was safely in British waters, he pulled back on the power and entered the port of Gibraltar as serenely as he had initially bid the port of Algeciras 'adios', as he didn't want to look like a Moroccan drug runner.

This kind of excitement or endeavour was what made Brian tick. He had traded a life of normality for one with more excitement many years earlier. A promising career as a commercial design artist had beckoned upon graduation but that clearly would never have satisfied Brian, despite his clear talent. A further step into film artwork with Pulfords Advertising and Amalgamated Press did little to quell his itchy feet. A stab at West End coffee bar ownership ended when it was refused a liquor licence, limiting its business to daytime hours. A marriage to Dora, an attractive Athenian, and subsequent move to Greece to start a life together lasted six years. Her disapproving brothers were held in check by a strong patriarch, who enjoyed a better relationship with his new son-in-law than his daughter ever did. But within days of his father–in-law passing away, Brian was brusquely escorted to Athens airport and handed a one-way ticket at gunpoint. Brian obliged as that was a little too rich, even for his adventurous blood!

In Greece he had enjoyed running nightclubs and beach resorts when he wasn't racing power boats, which was very much more his kind of thing. When he had crashed a power boat onto the judge's trestle table during an event in Glyfada it had made the local press in Athens. Managing a travelling entertainments troupe around American army bases circling the Mediterranean further whet his appetite for travel. His involvement in the attempted robbery of a betting shop in the early 1960's provided a flash of excitement, the kind of addictive stimulation Brian relished. But his arrest and subsequent 18 months he spent in Lewes prison put paid to any ambitions of career criminality. A £200 bribe by his furious Freemason father to the clerk of the court in Brian's case evidently had little effect on the outcome of the trial.

Offbeat people and places always appealed to Brian. Normal was boring and ordinary was stifling. Stealing your boat back from Spanish customs was the kind of normal he liked. And if you were to trace the story of how he came to be gliding into Gibraltar harbour with a caddish grin held across his incredulous and somewhat frightened face, you would have to go back to the start of the main chapter in the story of his life – the diving one… back to the dock in the east end of London in 1970, where he first found his calling. He wasn't going to be an artist, or a nightclub impresario or a power boat racer. He was going to become a commercial diver and help shape an offshore industry in its infancy.

"You made it then, Bri?" Bill confirmed, while sliding his friend a glass of well-earned cognac across the table of a Gibraltarian bar.

"Jesus, that got a bit hairy," he replied, with characteristic understatement, before taking a long sip.

02. Sink or Swim

"Fuck me! Look boys, it's George fucking Best," the dive boss mocked. He was sitting in a deck chair wearing a blue-collared shirt and grey slacks, with a knotted handkerchief as his chosen sunscreen. The two assistants, each with a flat cap, cigarette and weathered donkey jacket, stood either side of their 'Gaffer', drinking tea. All three had been there for four hours, waiting for the right candidate. Some would-be applicants had been rejected with a mixture of derisive grunts and a dismissive "fuck off, sunshine," before even reaching the dockside adjudication panel. In between the few applicants, their gaze had been drawn to the constant shift within the London docks. Ships were arriving from all corners of the globe and the contents were being hoisted onto the siding by mustard yellow dockside cranes. The dock workers were so numerous they looked like ants, and were each equipped with a gaff hook. Clouds of dust were rising from sacks containing all manner of commodities – flour and concrete and fertilizers. Timber and building materials shared the key side with frozen pig carcasses, piled high on wagons by aproned dockers.

Until Brian arrived that is.

He was back in the job market after accentuating the nipples of a female star on his last illustrated film poster a little too much for his boss and the film censors' liking. One of his many uncles, who was employed in the docks had told Brian about the advert about the 'experienced' diving job. He had checked out the advert stuck to the side of a van. The same uncle also knew Brian was mad enough to try and probably to get away with it too. He had sufficient easy charm and confidence to get himself in or out of whatever situation. All the berths in sight were occupied, apart from the one Brian approached. He was clean shaven, wearing sunglasses and smoking a cigarette – not the usual look in the docks. Neither was a tame pair of bell bottom trousers or his long-collared leather jacket. He had dressed casually for an informal recruitment process that Brian hoped would include neither a long line of applicants to outshine nor a criminal records check. In the silent judgement of the panel, he at least appeared to be in excess of 18 years old and to possess brain cells measured in double figures.

"Morning. I'm Brian. I'm here about the diving job you've got on the van up there?"

"And you're here for the diving are you?" the gaffer asked sarcastically, although Brian had made it further than any other hopeful.

"Yep."

"And experienced are 'ya?"

"Yep," Brian replied and grinned, masking his lie. His only 'experience' were school diving awards from various heights, some 25 years before.

The night before last a shipment of copper coils had fallen overboard, rendering the bay unusable for fully laden ships. For all the dive boss's mocking, the gaffer ideally had to get the dock floor cleared that day and needed to get someone in the water. But not just anyone. A few seconds passed with the gaffer's eyes squinting ever harder in confusion before he spoke: "OK boys, let's put him in a suit!" An abrupt discussion on payment was had while the dive assistants were summoned into action with a series of hand gestures from the gaffer.

Within ten minutes, Brian was out of his suave attire and sitting down in a rubber diving suit which fastened onto the curved breastplate that soon dropped over his head. Brian didn't have time to notice the numerous patch repairs on the suit as he was asked by an assistant, "Righto, step into these."

'These' were a pair of lead boots lashed endlessly around Brian's feet with lengths of shoelace and thin strips of salty leather. The assistants told Brian they were worn to aid buoyancy while wearing a suit that was inflated in its entirety when underwater. The breastplate then required an external jockstrap to secure it before a dive belt of 25kg was loaded around his waist, giving rise to thoughts of how he could even stand up, let alone walk to the timber ladder and down to the water. As the weight increased, so did his inward trepidation. The familiar sounds and hand gestures Brain attempted at each stage of the weight being loaded upon him weren't fooling everyone though.

For reasons of conscience or kindness, one assistant working closest to Brian whispered some rudimentary instructions among the more official commands, as he wasn't as easily fooled or desperate as the gaffer.

"Right, so the crane hook will be lowered down your descend line each time," the assistant then lowered his voice. *"Adjust the valve that you'll 'ave by 'ya left 'and for buoyancy when you get in."*

Each unofficial direction ended with a nod or a slight wink to confirm Brian understood. Brian nodded back but he didn't really understand as he had never dived before.

"The coils measure about six feet by ten feet and will be as thick as 'ya arm. So just hook it on to each coil as you find 'em. They reckon there are 20 of 'em down there. *You 'ave an exhaust valve in the 'elmet you can operate with 'ya chin,*" the assistant concluded. Brian nodded back again, very little the wiser.

A helmet cushion that looked like a padded toilet seat preceded the fitting of the brass helmet. Each side porthole was fixed: only the front was left open once the helmet was rotated onto the housing of the breastplate and locked into place. Inside, a tiny speaker crackled with the voice of the second assistant as he performed a check of the communications.

"Diver 1, are you receiving? Over."

"Yep. Can hear you fine."

"You meant 'Yes, topside' didn't you?" the second assistant said, although the correction was disguised as a question. "OK, check complete."

While closing the front porthole and sealing Brian in, he received his final uttered guidance, "OK, you're done. Now we'll stand you up and down the ladder into the water." A final double-tap on the crown of the helmet was his signal that he was clear to start working.

Brian tried to nod but he found he couldn't. He was helped to his feet and used all his strength to lift his feet, one roughly in front of the other, toward the ladder. Once he was turned around and climbing down and the air and comms cables were fed safely off the quayside, the assistants joined in operating the pump feeding Brian air below the surface. Although each had a cigarette seemingly glued to their mouths, they appeared more in need of air once the handles on the pump begun turning.

Brian felt the cold water through the suit immediately. The water pressure was acting to force the inside surface of the suit against whatever was inside. The water level reached the portholes then progressed past the crown of the helmet. Every step dropped him lower into an opaque brown soup until all three portholes were darkened by the murky estuarine potage. On the last step of the ladder, which Brian estimated was some three metres below the surface. It was time to take a leap of faith down the descend line. He could feel and see bubbles emanating from what appeared to be an alarming leak at the rear of his bulbous helmet – he wasn't to know this was normal. But he still stepped off, readying himself to play with the valves the assistant had tried to educate about.

As he descended the ten metres to the river bed, with his ears popping, he gave the valve by his left hand a generous twist and inflated the suit like a balloon, pushing the suit outwards against the pressure the water was exerting on him. With his knees evidently held higher in the suit than was designed, the legs inflated disproportionally with air which carried equal scents of diesel and cigarette smoke. This meant that, in mid-sinking, Brian was spun upside down. He watched his over-inflated legs arrest his descent and begin to rise back towards the surface as fast as the bubbles leaking from his helmet.

With the bubbles further obscuring his already limited vision from a 'leak' in his helmet he was still to learn was routine, he inelegantly surfaced in the empty dock like a bloated, beached whale.

The sight of this made the gaffer roll his eyes and left little doubt that Brian had overstated his ability to perform the task. But luckily this happened to be the moment when Brian started to get a feel for it. Next, he pushed against the chin valve to lower the pressure and buoyancy of the suit, taking him back below the surface, where his mistakes could remain private. Once he was submerged from view, the gaffer remarked sagely of his new 'experienced diver';

"Well, he'll either work it out or kill 'is-fucking-self."

If he wasn't an experienced diver as the advert desired, the gaffer had expected Brian to bottle it during the suiting-up process. But he didn't, his grin had just grown bigger and soon it had been too much trouble to get him back out of the suit.

Of course, the gaffer wouldn't have seen Brian plummeting to the bottom, into a blind soup of mud, sediment and sunken flotsam – some of which to was to be attached to the crane hook that followed a couple of minutes after Brian's second descent. The gaffer also didn't witness Brian nearly overinflating his suit a second time, as a bite on the exhaust chin valve saved further blushes.

But he did see Brian's next mistake... After battling through the two-metre layer of mud that constituted the river bed wearing lead boots that only seemed capable of pulling him deeper into, he managed to locate his first offending coil.

"OK topside, fist coil ready to lift," Brian confirmed and the crane driver was given a lift signal by the gaffer. Brian felt the crane cable start to tense and then lift the coil. And then he felt himself lift next to the coil, attached to the same hook under his arm and unable to free himself from making a second appearance on the surface. He had inadvertently attached himself to the crane hook. When he surfaced, the gaffer felt sure his prediction that Brian would kill himself, would come true.

Again and again, with the first five coils recovered from the berth, Brian was also attached. And with each return to the water off the end of a laden hook, he refused to look towards the quayside to give the gaffer a chance to wave his arms around and call the operation off. Instead, he chose to demonstrate willingness to continue, in spite of the very apparent flaws in his technique. And he knew he was making progress, as did the gaffer, when he watched the sixth coil lift to the surface without him.

The dive gaffer held back on delivering his rebuke as Brian cleared 14 of the estimated 20 coils. He also waited until Brian had hauled himself and the extra 80kg back up the ladder onto the dock like a failed escapologist act. He waited even longer while his assistants removed the helmet, helmet cushion, weight belt, lead footwear, air supply and comms cables, breast plate, jockstrap and finally, the muddied dive suit.

"So, you're not experienced?"

Feeling light as a feather and pleased with his effort, Brian viewed the offending coils he had recovered, however inelegantly, before coming clean, "Not really."

"You cheeky bugger. I bloody thought so. Well you know you'll only get 'alf the 'ourly rate we agreed, sunshine."

"OK," Brain replied, annoyed but aware he could do little to effect this statement.

"But I like the fact you carried on. You persevered and I like that a lot."

Brian took that as rhetorical so just pulled on a well-earned cigarette and waited for the gaffer to continue.

"So, if you wanna came back in the morning?"

"Yeah?" Brian answered, "Yeah, I could come back in the morning."

"And I'll pay you the full rate that we agreed this morning because you're experienced now!"

Brian left the berth and his new colleagues wearing the same half-smirk with which he had arrived. He also had a ticket to scrabble around in a layer of river swill deeper than he was, but for full pay. Unbeknown to Brian as he headed for the pub to buy his uncle a drink, the gaffer had just given him entry into the emerging global industry of commercial diving. And he would dive a lot deeper than the bottom of the Thames.

Oil and gas platforms were springing up in the North Sea like mushrooms following the discovery of oil in the '*Forties*' field in 1970. But Brian's first diving job was to be in more exotic locations than that. And he was fine with that. The hydro-carbon heyday of North Sea would come in time.

03. Borneo Beckons

With the invitation back to clear the berth of the remaining copper coils came the experience that Brian lacked. And the increase to full pay was most welcome. It made for a daily wage attractive enough to draw Brian back for more scrabbling around in the mud. Commercial diving was in its embryonic stage. The leap from civil engineering diving required a whole new technology that Brian increasingly absorbed himself in. It was a young industry so it unavoidably had a 'trial and error' approach to safety.

Then there was the ever present danger of, and ongoing efforts to avoid decompression sickness, or 'The Bends'. 'The diver's disease' was a potentially lethal condition caused by dissolved gasses in the blood stream re-forming into relatively inert bubbles, but with the ability to travel, and thereby to affect any part of the body. The bloodstream absorbs more of the gases as the external pressure increases. Symptoms of this dreaded condition would vary from a superficial skin rash to something more permanent like paralysis or death. Depending on the working depth of the diver, the ascent to the surface would be staggered at 'decompression stops' to allow the body to absorb the blood-borne gases at a manageable rate.

His first overseas posting swapped the Brown Windsor soup-like visibility of the estuarial Thames for the warmer climes of the Arabian Gulf. Its waters were like a warm winter bath and clear as consommé. The heavy rubber suit and diver's helmet were exchanged for a swimming trunks and more modern scuba equipment for another salvage job. While sipping a final cognac during the landing in Dubai, Brian was unable to distinguish where the desert ended and the sand runway began. Baking hot, dry and dusty, Brian didn't put down roots in the Gulf. He rarely did this anywhere. His heart was always in Essex with his immediate family, but his head and the rest of his body followed where the money was at the time. And with OPEC threatening to turn off the taps and cause a global oil shortage, each nation was keen to break their reliance on foreign oil and was thus willing to ramp up their own drilling concerns, be they on land or in deep water offshore. And if they were offshore, that's where commercial divers came in.

After exploration and discovery of tell-tale oil deposits, the rush was on for energy independence and no budget was too big. Large petrochemical companies won exploration licences at knockdown prices and further favourable terms were offered once the scale of the find was known. Rigs had to be fabricated and then towed out to the oilfield and strategically sunk in place or piles driven into the seabed and a drilling platform lowered onto the top. Despite the design varying they all had one thing in common – they had to get the crude ashore to be refined. So pipelines, sometime hundreds of kilometres in length had to be laid to get the 'black gold' to the refinery. After Dubai came a short posting to New Zealand, into the depths of the west coast of the North Island, where oil had first been discovered a century before by evidence of natural seepage. On a windless day, an oily sheen could be observed on the surface of the ocean from the beaches of the town of New Plymouth. And now the machines with the ability and men with the knowhow were arriving to extract it.

The next posting brought him a little closer to home and upped his experience even further. In Borneo, he swapped an oil rig bunk for a humid riverside house on stilts, where a constant stream of almond-eyed locals ferried past in makeshift narrow boats. Palm trees lined his abode and rang with insect cries after dark. And New Zealand's Taranaki oilfield was exchanged for the Badak gas field in the Macassar Strait in Eastern Kalimantan. It was a thankful return to warmer diving conditions than those he had experienced in the cool, wild Tasman Sea.

The formality of oilrig life was replaced by the informality of the pipe-laying vessel, *Benbecula*. The wide-based tug had been converted to lay a pipeline that came in fifty metre lengths with a diameter of 50cm. These had to be welded together on the seabed by divers working in shifts. The eight crew of the *Benbecula* looked more like a gaggle of pirates than the highly skilled group they were. On the rust- and grease-covered deck, close to the main structure of the living quarters and bridge, there was a tubular compression chamber. It was three metres in length and a cramped one and a half metres in diameter, while its white powder-coated exterior was stained with vertical rust trails from the oxidization of the rivet heads sealing the door assembly or mountings of the control panel and dials. A working depth of twenty metres necessitated a slow ascent of a minute per five metres of depth, then a further few minutes held at a five metre depth, before the final appearance on the surface. The compression tank was only on board for use in an emergency to reverse the bends if a diver had to be recovered due to an accident.

The normal dive supervisor had been struck down by dysentery, necessitating a promotion within the ranks and Brian had got the job. From beneath a ragged blue tarpaulin, hastily erected by lashing random poles at each corner to guard the communication equipment in the raging monsoon downpours, Brian found a wooden box to sit on and took a step up the ladder. Shaving his new moustache was troublesome in such primitive conditions, so he had allowed a full beard to grow. Along with swimming shorts, sandals and a white headset, he wore a tan leather jacket over his shoulders to protect against the balmy driving rains. Over the course of a working day, many topics were discussed during the diving that was continuing beneath the deck. At one point, the sex lives of the crew while offshore, a grandiose term for the extracurricular acts offered by the short Asian man who washed their underpants, was up for debate.

"Jesus, really?" Brian recoiled, on learning of a base behaviour that seemed common among his fellow shipmates, that of violating the laundry boy, in the absence of any via female stock. This band of feral brothers were importing the sexual revolution to Borneo and it was taking root.

"Yeah, we all have a go." Came the reply from twenty metres.

"Dirty baastards! Mind you, there ain't much action around here so I might join you one day," Brian joked, his incredulous eyes dampened by amused tears. "Anyway diver one, how is your air now?"

"I got 100 bar of pressure left, topside," came the crackly reply.

"Will you have enough to finish or do I send another diver down, diver one?"

"No, I got enough. I'm nearly done, topside."

"Magic. The weather is closing in so you'll be the last in the water. We have to head to *'the beach'*." This was the slang for a return to harbour.

With the return of diver one, Brian's ramshackle structure on the stern of the deck was stood down, the beers were cracked opened and the joints were puffed on. Their imminent return to shore and all the pleasures that awaited them, sins denied to them on board, the poor laundry boy aside, was also something to celebrate. That the trip had been curtailed by bad weather was also cause for celebration, as they still got paid. Brian also had an appointment he would rather keep.

Unfortunately, the dive company had other plans for their vessel and Brian couldn't find an excuse to refuse them. Much against the will of the crew, the company had booked an extra decommission job closer into shore where *Benbecula* could still operate. So, next morning, the deflated and very inebriated crew assembled on deck and headed for the abandoned remnants of an oilrig.

The delirious dive supervisor was still in his berth, racked by body sweats and intestinal explosions, so supervision of this additional task also fell on Brian's shoulders. He had been informed that the dynamite, wiring and detonators they would use to shear the piles just above the seabed would be sent out on a tug. But Brian had no experience of explosives other than having successfully avoided them throughout the London Blitz and neither did the remaining members of his crew.

There were eight piles to sink, in parallel lines of four. The structure they once supported had been removed by a barge crane and scrapped some months prior. Now just eight rapidly corroding stilts remained, each standing some fifteen metres clear of the surface. A further forty metres was hidden from view below. Once *Benbecula* was anchored into position, Brian gripped the supports of the diver's cradle and joked with his crew mates as he was hoisted out clear of the side of *Benbecula* and lowered down for an inspection dive. Diver one accompanied his supervisor into the water by simply jumping in next to Brian. The visibility was good, the temperature was as warm as a hot-spring and the water was teeming with sea life. There may have been equivalent lifeforms in the Thames docks, only Brian hadn't been able to see them. And when in the water, that is how Brian preferred it. He preferred not to be able see what was out there.

A rudimentary poke around on the seafloor to assess the job, interrupted by the visit of a leatherback turtle, brought about a return to the cradle for Brian. While waiting for the cradle to start lifting, he peacefully floated horizontally watching diver one ascend through clouds of his own expended air. The sun shimmered through the surface and the euphoric effects of nitrogen narcosis were not unpleasant, although they could easily lead to overconfidence. Simple cognitive questions were repeatedly asked by supervisors of their divers to measure the effects of this condition on the diver. But if managed properly by an experienced diver, it was much the same as feeling momentarily drunk with all the misplaced boldness that engenders.

This rare moment of solitude, which wasn't possible up on deck, cemented how much Brian loved the path he had chosen. It was only ever beautiful down there and he loved his job and his existence. The pay also helped and later that day he would be blowing something up. But why couldn't he just stay down here, he thought.

The dynamite duly arrived by tug and was gingerly moved onto the open deck of *Benbecula*. They weren't aware that they had been provided with an amount which was considerably in excess of what was required. So they simply divided the total eight times and then each batch was attached to one of the piles a metre above the seabed. They worked through the day, manoeuvring the dive boat close to each of the piles in turn, thinking it unsafe for diver one to descend with all the dynamite. With the coastline now tantalisingly visible on the not-too-distant horizon, the crew were, to a man, in a rush to complete their delayed return to port so no one disagreed with this approach. Overkill simply seemed a better approach than having to repeat the process.

Benbecula was suitably retired by her skipper to a safe distance. Long detonation wires had been attached in a circuit between each batch of dynamite and a twist detonator, that Brian held in the palm of his left hand. With all eyes fixed on the protruding piles in the near distance and Brian, he took a furtive look over his shoulder, smiled and twisted the handle in his right hand anti-clockwise. A second passed, which was long enough for Brian and some of the crew to think it hadn't worked and he gazed down at the detonator. Then suddenly, BOOM!

The water around the piles lifted first into irregular columns of ice white foam before the first of the eight piles was launched into the tropical, cloud-laden sky. Each of the crews' mouths were agape and their necks were bent backwards to fully absorb the spectacle. One by one, as they had been wired in sequence, the supports lifted clear of the bay like a multiple Cape Canaveral launching. Their landings created equal amounts of terror and awe. Once the spectacle was nearly complete, the crew's gaze eventually returned to Brian, with enquiring looks on each of their faces.

His jaw jutted out guiltily as he watched the last of the rig piles re-enter the atmosphere.

"We might have dropped a right bollock there, guys. I think we may have overdone that," he commented sagely before quickly continuing to block any possible replies: "Right, shall we get back to the beach now? I have a date to get to."

COMEX

131, av. Joseph-Vidal, 13 - Marseille-8e.
Tél. 77.51.77

RECRUTE POUR SON DÉPARTEMENT PLONGÉE PROFONDE :

* *Techniciens, bac technique, dessinateurs ou ouvriers spécialisés ayant plusieurs années stabilité dans même entreprise.*

* *Age 25 à 32 ans.*

* *Plongée : niveau 1er échelon minimum.*

* *Si possible célibataires ou aptes à nombreux déplacements à l'étranger.*

* *Anglais parlé très souhaitable.*

* *Si vous ne remplissez pas ces conditions, ne nous écrivez pas.*

04. Aquanaut

Aquanaut:

Noun; A person who lives or works underwater.

An aquanaut is the undersea equivalent of an aeronaut or astronaut, who earn their corn within and outside our atmosphere respectively. The deeper parts of the ocean are as much as a mystery as the lunar surface and most hostile environment on planet earth.

1974 closed with Brian finishing up in Asia on the *Benbecula* and applying for a position with a French company called Comex, who specialized in deep offshore diving. Founded by Henry Delauze, a charismatic Marseille-based diving pioneer, they were considered the best in the business by oil companies and divers alike. A working relationship with the Swiss watchmaker Rolex for testing their timekeeping products at real-world depths, saw each new diver issued with their own Submariner timepiece. With 'COMEX' stamped on the face just below the centre pin, it was the only dedicated watch issued by the maker other than the type produced for NASA employees. With ongoing operations in the Gulf of Mexico, West Africa and now the North Sea, the demand for commercial divers was greater than ever. The fatality rate of the profession also lent extra impetus to Comex recruiters, the previous year had seen ten divers killed and numerous others retired from the industry through injury or incapacity. Few divers left the industry voluntarily.

SALVAMAR – A TALE OF SALVAGE & DEEP DIVING

In the science and engineering led boom that followed the discovery of oil and gas deposits in the North Sea, cut-price licences for oil companies with the means of extraction were thrown out by the Government like confetti. Thereafter the revenues would fuel a more prosperous and energy-independent country. So the race was on to get the resources ashore to refineries that also needed to be constructed, as did the drilling platforms and the pipelines that would eventually connect the two.

A move closer to home would have been preferable for Brian, but the UK was a depressing place to reside at the time. The economy was on its knees with union-led industrial action, leading its unfortunate nickname of the 'sick man of Europe'. The Irish Republican Army (I.R.A.) had shifted their campaign of terror against the colonisation of Northern Ireland from military targets in Ireland to indiscriminate attacks on the British mainland. Brian was now an uncle five times over with the difficult arrival of second nephew to his younger sister, Colleen. The last update he had received on the newborn had revealed that he was confined to an incubator with a suspected hole in the heart.

Although Brian's travel lust was strong and yet to be fully satisfied, his bond with his family wasn't to be underestimated. He was of coarse cockney stock from a tightly woven net of uncles and aunties and cousins. With the passage of life, he had become an uncle five times over. Birthdays and particularly Christmas were big familial events, especially with four nephews and one niece, he attended when he could and enjoyed very much when he did so. However, he also had a life to live to the full.

Brian was invited to attend a training course with Comex at their training base outside Aberdeen. Along an undulating country lane beside a trickling brook, stood a two-storey Georgian house with a tall chimney marking each corner and a central dormer window in the lead-lined roof. Symmetrical windows across the front were repeated in the back, while the ground floor was given over to compression chambers, gas bottles and training equipment. The bright first floor rooms had been converted into makeshift classrooms and afforded generous views of the tree-lined lake below. The algae-shaded cab of a dredging machine stood proud of the still surface, the result of a botched attempt at dredging the lake to enable training dives. But as the dredging plant had got sunk into the mud, something it was specifically designed to avoid, the sensible decision was made to abort the idea, as divers would have become plugged before they were waist deep in water.

Along with other interested divers from all corners of the globe, Brian was sat at his own melamine desk, one of twenty around the smoky office space, each with their ashtray. After brief introductions from all attending it became clear who sat where in terms of experience. Brian was older than the average, having misspent his youth in the eyes of many, but certainly not his own.

He was 37 years old at the time and looking at a short career in the North Sea as the cut off age for commercial divers was 40. He took notes on a small sketch book when not smoking a cigarette. Rhodesians, South Africans, Australians, Belgians, Welshman, Russians, Germans, Norwegians, Americans all gathered together to learn the techniques of saturation deep diving. Scottish was the most common British accent in the classroom but the language most often spoken was French.

Georges was the instructor: he had a generous nose and narrow eyes, a tank top and shirt with lengthy collars –

his only defence against Aberdeen's version of late spring. Under a nicotine-stained suspended ceiling, they were taught the principles of this diving method. Most were proficient at air diving and all had the required knowledge of decompression stops. They were familiar with diving masks and scuba tanks. But now they learnt about proper dive support vessels with a crew numbered in three figures, the helium/oxygen gas mixtures, the compression chambers, the bell transfers, the diving suits fed hot water to combat hypothermia, the communications equipment, common underwater structures they would encounter, the pressures of working depths and the known potential hazards – although new and numerous ways to die were continually being discovered.

"And please don't be surprised when you take your first breath of heliox gas in the chamber, and you sound like a fucking canary bird!" Georges warned with his Anglo-Franco pronunciation, to a round of laughter from his eager class. "The novelty wears off, believe me."

To congratulate his class on completing the theoretical part of the training on the first day, Georges, had four bottles of champagne and a pitted, rusty sword brought into the class to toast his new recruits. The petite French secretary brought a tray of crystal champagne glasses – she had caught Brian's eye on an earlier visit to the classroom – Georges pulled up the sash window and sabred the bottles of champagne out of the window. As though he was making a sweeping tennis backhand stroke, he ran the blade of the sword sharply up the neck towards the thick ring around the wired cork, followed by a column of bubbles. He repeated this Napoleonic flourish for each bottle, filling the remaining empty glasses once the bubbles had stopped erupting from the neck. When all the glasses were full, he raised his own in a toast to his class.

"Gentlemans, a warm welcome to Comex. We will continue tomorrow downstairs in the chambers."

The following morning, after retreating to their respective digs, the class assembled, all more comfortable with each other following the inevitable awkwardness of the first day. The space was colder than the classroom above, it smelt of diesel and faint sounds of Supertramp could be heard on a quiet radio. Georges was stood wearing a cardinal red diving suit and a yellow full body harness in front of a fully operational compression chamber, an L-shaped configuration of two interconnecting chambers. The horizontal portion was 1.8 metres in diameter, 6m long and painted powder blue, which was accurate to the size of chamber they would encounter in the North Sea, and separated into two compartments by an airlock. This allowed for the pressure in the unoccupied portion of the chamber to be adjusted down to normal atmospheric pressure or increased to match the operating pressure exerted in the occupied portion. The principles of compression and decompression could be demonstrated by movement of divers between the divide. The transfer under pressure into the bell and exit was simulated by the vertical chamber, its lower portion flooded to mimic the exit from and return to the bell itself.

"Gentlemans, Welcome back. Jolly good to see you again. I see none of have thrown in the towel, as you say. I trust you had a good evening? Some of you maybe a bit too good an evening by the looks of things," Georges could see some of his scholars had overindulged the previous evening, as some were squinting and noticeably more unshaven compared to the first day. "If some of you are feeling, how you say, queasy, please don't puke in the helmet when you put it on as you will most likely drown. So be careful, *oui*?" His blunt warning came as enough of a shock to sober up a few on the spot.

Georges continued to explain the suit he was wearing and the canary yellow diver's helmet that was displayed on a table beside him, "This is the latest diving suit, you may all be aware this is a wet suit? *Oui*? And through your umbilical, which we will get to later this morning, is fed an oxygen helium gas mixture, Hydrox or heliox for example, into your helmet and hot water into this suit. The same as you will be breathing in the living chamber. The yellow harness is worn to make a recovery easier. The helmet weighs twenty-five kilograms approximately. Our bells are fitted with 50 metre umbilicals for each diver, which is about a hundred and fifty of your feets. Without this lifeline, the estimate before hypothermia sets in at the bottom of the North Sea is four minutes." As the facts sunk in, the lethargy of the class evaporated.

"And you control the flow of water to the suit?" Brian asked, interrupting Georges.

"Good question. No, the flow is controlled by the whoever stays in the bell, or 'bellman' as they are called. You can simply request more flow. Or less depending in the conditions of course. There should plenty of pressure available to overcome any ingress of cold water, even if the suit gets torn. Does that answer your question, Brian?"

"Yeah, magic, thanks."

"Are there any other questions?" He paused but no further questions were forthcoming, so he continued, "So the aim of the rest of the week is get you all familiar with the suit and chamber and the bell. You'll do a simulation dive in the vertical chamber you can see behind me with an experienced diver as the bellman. That is the vertical chamber that is sunk into the ground. If that all goes well then you will all be off to Norway next to dive in a fjord, on board *The Godmother*!"

Georges reached for the helmet and placed it over his head to explain how and where the all-important umbilical, a collection of air, water and communications pipes and wires twisted together and crudely held with gaffer tape at one metre intervals, was attached to the helmet. In that environment, without the umbilical you would be blind, unable to breathe and communicate with both the bellman and dive supervisor on the dive support vessel you are ultimately attached to. The only survival mechanism was a small scuba tank on the divers back known as the 'bailout', which was rich in oxygen, but only contained a five to seven minutes' supply, enough to support a return to the diving bell.

Diving work on the rigs or dive ships would be surface-orientated initially, by way of a scuba tank, face mask and crane operated cradle to transport the diver to and from their working depth. Those who were judged competent enough during saturation training would thereafter progress into the compression chambers. Each day spent inside the 'pot' paid an extra 'saturation' bonus, supplementary to the regular day rate and stints of four to six weeks in saturation weren't uncommon.

Not counting the simulation of the diving bell mock-up, Brian did his first deep bell dive in south west Norway from *The Godmother*, a pontoon attached to cables either side of the fjord to enable the vessel to easily traverse the body of water, which offers different depths for training purposes.

As with a performer about to take to the stage, the descent always raised the trepidation levels. But Brian always thought that if he was a little nervous, then he was paying attention. He had hung back on arrival, wanting others to go before him so he could learn from their common mistakes.

"*The Godmother* is a pontoon, so it's very stable. You find out on the job that the smaller the vessel, the greater the surface movement, which affects how the bell will behave." The instructor was making small talk while the claustrophobic bell descended to the bottom of the frigid fjord, sounding like a Bee Gee.

"Magic," Brian replied sounding much the same as a chipmunk. He struggled to stifle a chuckle as it felt absurd to be having a normal conversation about life or death matters while sounding like a pair of sopranos.

The bell stopped 100m below *The Godmother*, an estimated 10m above the fjord bed. The steady nature of the pontoon meant a stable bell beneath, unlike the unforgiving swells frequently visited upon the North Sea that awaited him. After unlocking and opening the heavy bell door, in the centre of the base of the bell, the instructor began releasing the coils of umbilical stored inside the bell, ready to feed to his diver.

"OK diver one. Are you ready?"

Brian nodded in nervous instinct, his jutting jaw hidden in his helmet, before realising the instructor was only seeking a thumb and index finger 'OK' sign in response.

"I just want you to leave the bell and search around on the bottom to the extent of your umbilical? OK?"

The lights outside the bell illuminated the surface lapping just below the exit into an alluring shimmer. Brian didn't exhibit any fear and climbed down the foot rungs through the narrow bell door into the unknown, while the instructor continued to feed his umbilical.

05. Bell

The oil boom in Aberdeen meant the social circuit loomed large with brash, overpaid ex-pats. The sex industry in the 'granite city' boomed as divers finally set free from the restraints of decompression chambers, returned to the 'beach' with a bottomless budget that could afford the highest of high class fire-breathing hookers. Most of the relationships the divers were in prior to working in the North Sea dissolved soon after, in the face of such competition. Exotic cars filled the car parks of local pubs and helicopter transfer hangars in this bubble of oil wealth.

Brian was in his second year in the North Sea when a keen new diver joined the group for his first stint in saturation – high on the thrills and money that awaited him. Brian guessed Mickey, with his long hair and ebullient smile, was in his mid-twenties, nearly fifteen years his junior. At least Mickey could speak English. A placement with a French or Belgian diver who couldn't speak a word of English had happened before. Mickey was keen to supplement his inexperience with tales from the comparative veterans around him. Brian obliged with a tale from his own first stint on the *Smit Lloyd 112*;

"I was sent out here for the first time two weeks after a double fatality, which I only found out afterwards."

"Fuck!" said Mickey

"Anyway, I was at fifty feet on a surface feed and we had this job to oversee the placement of a 50-ton ballast rock to one of the legs of a rig. So I'm halfway down and the crane operator decides to release the rock above me." Mickey's eyes widened as Brian continued, "all I felt was it brush past my temple as it dropped. It knocked me out cold and I dropped another 30 feet and hung on my airline. They got me back up on deck but had to decompress me properly in a chamber. That's the next thing I remembered, sunshine!"

"Jesus, Brian. You could have been a 'goner'," Mickey said, wide-eyed. His dysphonic voice carried an equal measure of exhilaration and instinctive fear.

Pilots don't speak of crashing, while astronauts never contemplate their fate while perched on top of a gigantic canister of gas sending them towards the stars. Brian could and would discuss his profession sparingly with his peers, but he actively sought to keep his own family in the dark on a lot of his exploits. This was because they lived very different lives, so they could never understand his world, also so that younger nephews and cousins didn't follow him into the lethal industry. It was mainly new recruits who revelled in the danger. Brian had himself when he started. He still loved the daily adrenaline surge of leaving the bell into the unknown.

Smit Lloyd 112 was a 65m long dive support vessel whose imposing bow sloped down to a flat, pontoon-like stern. Half the craft was given over to a working deck, dominated by the ships bridge that sandwiched between two towering exhaust funnels amidships. Brian could remember his first helicopter flight out to *Smit Lloyd 112* in the summer of 1975. The fascination of the flight since lost in the routine of repetition. It was early evening and the gas flare on the flame stack of a nearby drilling platform was as bright as the crimson sun that hung low in the sky. The sea had a welcoming lethargy, nothing like the monster waves that visited over the winter months.

The white paintwork of the helicopter was stained pink as it lifted up off the helipad, Aberdeen-bound, with the diving team Brian and his colleagues were replacing.

He had grown used to how his body looked after eight hours in a wetsuit pumped full of hot water; like an albino prune. He was also used to the constant noise, whether he was based on a rig or dive vessel. The whir and vibration of the generators and pumps was unremitting. While compressed in a chamber within a dive support vessel, you could add the shift of the sea into the equation. And after time, veterans could read the weather conditions by the motion felt inside the chamber. The food tasted of nothing when the divers were saturated: even the hottest curry was barely able to register on the palate. He had to learn to shit on command, as holding it in for an eight-hour shift caused understandable discomfort. Once the bowels have been purged, a dive support technician was requested to kindly pull a lever on the outside of the chamber so the high-pressured excrement could be withdrawn. Compared to life back on land, nothing was normal about this existence: cramped up in a pressurized metal tube with three or four other divers for twenty-eight days at a time, all of whom sounded like cartoon characters. Add to this the fact that your next shift on the bottom of the North Sea could be your last, if things went wrong. Absolutely nothing was normal about this existence.

The living quarters, where they socialised and had their meals, looked more like the inside of a cylindrical caravan, with burly frames perched on narrow seating crammed around a slender table. One aspect Brian never grew accustomed too was the decompression at the end of the term spent in saturation. Decompression was the worst part of the four-week period. Depending on the working depth prior to decompression, it normally translated into three to five days spent in a metal tube, without a single minute of the monotony being interrupted by another shift. It was just cards, oxygen mask, backgammon, put your oxygen mask back on, peruse a pornographic magazine, more oxygen and tasteless meals fed through the airlock. And repeat.

If you had received bad news like the death of a loved one or suffered an injury that required medical treatment onshore and had to leave early, you were stuck in there regardless. Unless you wanted decompression sickness, that is. And when you finally escape decompression, your hearing is attuned to the effects of helium, so the first few sentences sound like Barry White in the inner ear. After breathing inert gases for weeks, the nose is unprepared for the cacophony of aromas that shoot up the nostrils. Diesel, body odour, rotten fish, salt, rust, cigarette smoke and cooking fat from the kitchens would invade his nostrils.

Immediately after construction in June 1975, the *Smit Lloyd 112* had been converted from its original purpose of anchoring oil rigs to a dive support vessel stationed in the Argyll oil field. The field was in the British sector of the North Sea, three hundred kilometres east of any evidence of Scottish shoreline, on the same latitude as Edinburgh and Copenhagen. At a working depth of 80m, 12m shy of the summit of Big Ben, it held the distinction of being the first oil field to send its black gold ashore to be refined: a coffee coloured elixir that was sorely needed to help the 'sick man of Europe' recover.

The initial twenty-four hours working time had been sacrificed to anchoring *Smit Lloyd 112* into position above the worksite, delaying the group of divers' entry into the compression chamber. The extra time, when not hauled up in the cabin of the main deck, was spent performing equipment checks. The cabin was wallpapered around the rusty portholes; a patterned vinyl tablecloth was fastened down with drawing pins to a small rectangular table that was screwed into the wooden floor. Among the ashtrays, whiskey bottles and spent cups of tea sat Mickey, Geoff and Brian. Below their feet were the workings of a dive support vessel. Thousands of cylinders of oxygen and helium were stored securely in sturdy racking. Connected to these were a maze of feeder pipes, each with an arrow label to indicate the direction of flow; to or from the compression chamber. A control room was awash with dials which were used to read the pressures exerted within the three separate chambers, all interconnecting with a central area where the divers would suit up and transfer into the diving bell, once it was locked onto the pressurized living quarters. Thereafter, they were at the mercy of the dive supervisor to monitor the well-being of his divers.

Geoff, who had a moustache-less beard only around his broad jawline, was Brian's constant dive partner since starting on the *112* together. They had dived some 2000 hours together. Comfortable in one another's company, they had socialised a similar number of hours back in Aberdeen. Owing to his surname of Winton, Geoff claimed to be an original descendent of the founders of Winchester, his hometown, which was just inland from the southern shores of England. This always amused Brian, who had no such claims of breeding. In his late twenties and a fellow rolling stone (albeit a better spoken one), Geoff didn't like to debate the dangers of the industry and generally steered the conversation onto the benefits of the remuneration for such hardships.

"Did you order a car, Bri?"

"Yeah. I ordered the Maserati. I pick it up at the factory when we finish our hitch."

"Wow man," Mickey interjected. He always seemed interested in whatever his new peers were discussing. "What one? The Bora?"

"The Merak. The new one with the smaller engine."

"Wow. I can't wait to start earning some proper bread, man. What colour, Brian?"

"Nero black with brown leather interior."

Their downtime which was abruptly ended. The *112* had secured its final anchor and was ready to become operational so it was time for Mickey, Geoff and Brian to enter the chamber. The rusty hinge on the cabin door squawked open to reveal a short flabby man with ape-like limbs and a blank countenance. It was their authoritarian diving supervisor, a bilious Norwegian called Kaare. He was an emotionless yes-or-no-switch of a man who considered compromise a virtual defeat. By contrast, Brian was more of a creative "let's try it this way" person.

"Straighten yourselves up guys. Anyone not out on deck in 15 minutes will be fired!"

Mickey politely stood from the table to introduce himself to his new boss, but Kaare had said all he needed to and was already walking back to the control room, leaving the door ajar just as he had opened it.

"He seems a right cunt, that bloke," Mickey observed, his pride somewhat bruised.

Brian didn't verbally concur, choosing a silent form of agreement by knowingly raising his eyebrows as he cleared his section of table. He then stood and began to close his beige field jacket. Brian had drawn his name in bubble lettering across the flap closure on the left breast pocket, either side of the snap fastener. He had worked out it was best to just smile and agree to do it Kaare's way, only to revert to his original plan when he was under the water, citing some obstacle that invalidated Kaare's method statement. Unless it was an emergency, you were effectively your own boss down there. Unless a shark wanted to take a bite out of you, that is.

Kaare searched all three of his divers for booze and cigarettes before they were condemned to the chamber for the next four weeks. From a squeaky chair in the control room, Kaare then started to 'press down' his divers to the equivalent working depth they would be stored for the duration. The very first breath of helium set the vocals chords up to the highest octave. This was always a novelty for new divers, and Mickey was no exception.

The purpose of their first dive was to inspect and take photographs of a suspected leak on a wellhead manifold. Brian and Geoff briefed their eager new colleague on how the dive would be conducted. Brian would be Bellman, Geoff would be Diver One and Mickey Diver Two. Cruelly, through a series of winks and fin gestures, unseen by Mickey, Bellman and Diver One overlooked to inform Diver Two of the three-metre shark that frequently visited the site. Both Geoff and Brian had undergone the same heartless initiation as new divers and now it was Mickey's turn to find out for himself. To maintain this tradition was the only right and proper thing to do. Descending in the bell, after breaking the surface and shifting around in the splash zone, the divers felt the switch in power. A reversal of roles. On the surface divers were looked after and pampered. But descending to the workplace instantly changed that. Now they had to do their job. And everything and everyone aboard the vessel they dangled underneath was geared to assist them.

The bell slowed to a stop five metres above the sea floor, its metal walls dripping with condensation caused by the sea temperature of four degrees outside the bell. Diver Two would exit the bell first and was fitting his helmet while Geoff helped Brian unlock and then lift the 75kg bell door. There Mickey stared at the 60cm wide aperture into the unknown, the exterior bell lights illuminating the water immediately outside the exit. Brian stood ready to feed Mickey's umbilical and gave Diver Two his signal to exit. Mickey awkwardly stepped down the ladder into a dense shoal of shimmering cod.

"Good luck, Mickey" Brian said to himself with a wicked grin fixed across his face as Geoff kept watch through the bell window for signs of the shark.

06. Maserati

"*Bonjourno, Signore Worley*. Welcome to-*ah* the '*Casa el Tridente*'. Please-*ah* follow me-*ah*?"

"Magic."

Wearing a heavily starched suit, the oily looking Maserati salesman shook Brian's hand at the entrance of the car factory, below the curved sign that carried the car makers name and its evocative three pointed emblem of Neptune's trident, a prestigious marque of the rich and famous. While Ferraris were bought with newly acquired wealth, Maserati was the choice of the more understated old-money set. A series of eight brick hangars was terraced into two symmetrical banks of four, either side of a tarred central driveway, through which snaked a train track which was used to move materials around the plant. Despite Brian's best efforts to dress smartly for the morning appointment, the salesman was so well turned out in his suit and immaculately buffed shoes, he felt a little underdressed in his black shirt and cream bellbottoms. He had ordered the new Maserati Merak, a mid-engined 2 + 2 sports car, named after a star from the constellation Ursa Major. Ordering it through a dealership in the UK would have been boring. So would taking a test drive.

His new car had been prepared for its new customer and sat in the morning sun at the doorway of one hangar which was used to store finished vehicles before they were collected or shipped off around the world. From each roof strut supporting the long double-pitched

Gembrel roof hung a shaded fluorescent tube which threw light on the stone slab floor and various models awaiting their new owners. Each small pane of the factory windows around every hangar and even those in the gables had been blanked out with whitewash. The local birds were doing overtime, extending the dawn chorus into the late morning, with cheeping insects on backing vocals.

The diminutive salesman opened the sloping door with his slender fingers to reveal the interior, slightly disorientated by the sale of a right hand drive model. Every detail inside matched what Brian had ordered. The compact cassette quadrophonic stereo, weirdly located in the dashboard under the gauge cluster, between the steering column and the door. The honey brown leather covering the smooth seat bolsters and ribbed supports for the back and thighs. The rear seats, upholstered in the same matching hide and so shallow they could better be described as shelving than seating. He smirked as he realised he had a number of suitably sized nephews that would just fit and would love a ride in their uncle's new sports car. Anyone older would need to be folded in half in order to fit.

He signed the paperwork stooped over the roof as the bonnet sloped off below knee level, with a pop-up headlight either side. Brian's squared Aviator sunglasses, horseshoe moustache and hair that reached his eyebrows and collar reflected in the flawless black paintwork. His skin was still pale, fresh from another four weeks spent in a compressed metal tube. All around the car's bodywork there were bulges and scoops and a set of flying buttresses swooped each side from the roof line of the cabin to the car's rear, over of the slatted engine cover. Directly behind the leather rear shelves and in front of the back wheels was a French derived V6 power unit, the reliability of which would lead to regular costly entries in the service manual. It was a book Brian would become too familiar with for his liking, let alone his bank manager.

"*Grazie, Signore Worley*. Thank you-*ah* very much! Are you-ah driving to-*ah Inghilterra*?" The salesman was riding at the edge of his knowledge of the English language.

"England?"

"*Sì*. I mean yes-*ah*."

"No. To Marseille."

"Ah, *bellissimo*. You know-*ah* the way-*ah*?"

"No!" Brian replied, rather amused. "Not yet."

"*Ah*, OK. I get-*ah* you map? *Sì?*"

"Magic."

While waiting for the map, Brian placed his briefcase in the 'boot' under the front bonnet and then sat in the soft driver's seat. He leant forward from the squat seat and turned the key the salesman had already placed in the ignition barrel. A whirring metallic bray erupted behind him, transmitting through his seat and filled the cabin. With the salesman approaching, a map fluttering in his grasp, Brian lowered the electric window.

"*Ciao, Signore Worley!*" shouted the salesman as Brian left the engine running.

From the undulating road, vineyards and olive groves nestled below honeycomb stone hilltop villages. It was a perfect setting for Brian to enjoy his new toy. Summer smells of jasmine flowers and hot, dry grass carried on the wind into the cabin. His cigarette smoke soon cancelled that out, as did the mixture of burning oil, unspent fuel and scorching paint that ensued. Then the heat from the engine temperature began to rise. On a northern Italian morning, in the Emilia-Romagna region in August, the asthmatic air-conditioning couldn't compete. Neither could the stereo defeat the blare from the engine, just behind his seat. His target was Cassis, a port town holding its annual festival, sandwiched between steep cliffs of Cap Canaille, twenty kilometres east of Marseille. And his invite for the late afternoon had come from Anne, a slight French lady with short brown hair and bubble-high cheek bones who had been working for Comex in Aberdeen. So Brian's day had begun with an Italian breakfast and would conclude with a French dinner date.

He followed the route drawn on the map by the Maserati salesman, down to the coast via the Riviera di Levante and Riviera di Ponente, east and west of the port town of Genoa respectively. A short break to clear immigration at the French-Italian border was the only delay before the last leg down the Cote D'Azur, where he cut a dash through Monaco, Cannes and St Tropez.

He arrived at Budda Hermitage, Anne's parents elegant *maison de maître* style home, with some time spare, so he was introduced to the family: her brothers, the chic mother, the house guests and Anne's daughter, Kathleen. And Brian immediately hit it off with Maximilian, Anne's commodity surveying father, so he was offered a tour of the house by the head of the household. Maximilian dwelled around Brian's new car outside, telling his guest how impressed he was.

Vast crunchy gravel driveways were given dappled shade by the pine trees that lent a gentle voice to the shifting coastal winds. Under the trees and randomly placed gazebos, were sets of metal tables and slatted chairs, all white in colour. To one side of the main entrance was a swimming pool, and on the other side a tennis court. Each of the four floors of the residence had an abundance of guest facilities, reception rooms and balconies in a property with a footprint big enough to accommodate a shooting range in the basement. Unbeknown to Brian, while embracing Anne goodbye Maximilian had whispered in his daughter's ear just before they left for Cassis Marina, "why aren't you with Brian?" Her convex cheeks had flashed red before she had shot a glance over the top of her spectacles, acknowledging her father's endorsement.

Brian drove to the harbour as Anne only had a mini motorbike, not the most suitable means for transporting two adults and a six-year-old. "If you two jump out here and get us a nice table and I'll go and find a parking space."

But the owner of Bar Del La Marine had other ideas. While Brian was turning around to exit the harbour, he strode out from beneath navy blue and white striped awning that provided shade for his customers and stood in front of the Brian's bonnet while pointing to the area directly outside his restaurant.

"You park here!" he said most insistently, confident that such a glamorous looking car was good for business. The British number plate had suggested which language to use. Brian duly obliged.

SALVAMAR – A TALE OF SALVAGE & DEEP DIVING

Parked in Cassis harbour, his new car looked every bit as glamorous as the images in the brochure that had persuaded Brian to buy the Merak. All around the marina were shuttered windows with pot plants cluttering the sills and roofs of curved terracotta tiles. The whitewashed houses around the quay, whose narrow and deep forms were reflected in the glassy harbour waters were all either two or three storeys. The ground floor of each was either a bar or bistro, with tables arranged under canopies of differing hues and styles. Brian was falling in love with the place. With its steep-sided Calanaques just west of the harbour, the idea of ordering a boat soon seemed a fitting one. The sea was clear and azure, not the usual brown of the Essex coast. Later that night, it acted as a finely textured mirror for a fireworks display, choreographed to the music of Pink Floyd.

Brian couldn't understand a word that people were saying, but he liked the food and the *savoir faire*. His car fitted in the chic surroundings of the French Riviera, much more so than southeast Essex or the east coast of Scotland. He could let it all hang out in Cassis. If he tried the same back in Arbroath, it would get frostbitten. He was in his prime with a burgeoning bank account and a flash car and now he could look for an apartment that overlooked the whole scene: the yachts moored in the marina and the baroque castle precariously perched on a headland, marking the eastern limit of the town. The lifestyle and climate fitted him like a glove. Throw in a willing and flexible landlord who would allow substantial rental arrears to accumulate in Brian's absence and he could become a Cassis resident.

The IRA weren't bombing France and the three-day week was resulting in regular power cuts and bags of rubbish lying in the streets rather than being collected. The winter of discontent was approaching and the sick man of Europe was still a long way from a recovery. The capped working week seemed to have crippled the UK but France seemed to operate quite happily on roughly the same hours. A move to Cassis and the costs thereof could be written off by a creative accountant, on the grounds that the climate would reverse the effects of the Vitamin D deficiency the body suffers when enclosed in a metal tube.

After two years working for Comex, the expiration of his documents had coincided nicely with a long and well-earned summer break in the South of France. A diving medical, offshore survival and Non Destructive Testing (NDT) certificates were all in need of refreshing. A forgotten appointment here or delayed course start date there could easily add up to two or three months out on the beach. He was 39 and realistically only had a year left in the North Sea. So they would be his last set of registrations. He couldn't face another winter in Arbroath, where he had taken a small bungalow flat. It was kitted out with all the mod-cons; shag pile carpets, a PVC sofa that was capable of melting if exposed to direct sunlight, hanging chair, a bedside Teasmaid, slide projector, electronic typewriter, colour TV, HiFi music centre, record player and automatic coffee machine in the kitchen. But the view of a corn field, a continuous porridge coloured sky and conversations in his local pub revolving around catching and smoking mackerel, a local delicacy called an Arbroath Smokey, swiftly become tedious. The fondest memory of his time in Arbroath was smoking a cannabis joint with a fellow diver he was putting up and subsequently getting lost in the fog for five hours while attempting to visit his local shop for a much-needed sausage roll.

Kathleen had an ice cream, her mother a glass of wine and Brian sipped at a double cognac.

"Anne," Brian asked, "would it be easy to find an apartment here?"

"I do not see why not, *Bri-yon*," Brian liked the way she pronounced his name with her accent.

"I like it here. I'll take a look for a place tomorrow. Could you help with translating for me?"

Anne was only too happy to oblige. Her father would be overjoyed.

07. Newhaven

"Hi Pat. How's you? You OK?"

"Is that Brian? Lovely to hear from you, how are you?" Bill's flame haired wife, Pat, had answered the phone.

"I'm OK, Pat. How are you."

"Very well. Where are you now? Haven't heard from you for a while, have we?"

"I'm in Cassis in France, Pat. Near Marseille. Just rented a place here. But I'm back over in a few days to look at a boat down in Brighton."

"You wanna speak to Bill?"

"Yeah, Pat. Is he there?"

"Yeah, he's out in the garden, I'll go fetch him for you, Brian"

"Smashing. Thanks Pat. Look after yourself." Brian traced her audible steps out through the sliding French windows and heard them both return through them, talking about whatever Bill was busy with in the garden. Bill reached the phoned, jovial as ever and happy to revel in tales from his globe-trotting friend.

"Hello Mr Worley. How are you, sir?"

"Hi Bill. I'm good."

"It's been a while, bloody 'ell. What are you up to now, Bri?"

"I'm coming over this week. That's why I'm phoning."

"Oh, why's that Bri. Everything OK?"

"Yeah, magic. All is well. I'm coming to look at a boat later this week. Near Brighton."

"What you looking at, Bri?"

"It's a Princess 32. It's a year old. A friend of a friend I work with is selling. It's called '*Highroller*'."

"Blood-dy 'ell. You're a boy, ain't you? What a name. How's the Maserati?"

"I was gonna drive over, but the baastard's in being fixed."

"Not again, Bri."

"Don't remind me," Brian changed the subject onto the next object of his playboy desire. Bill also worked in the oil industry and got time off in large chunks like Brian. "If you have time, would be able to meet me there? Just so I've got another pair of eyes as you know more about boats than I do."

"Yeah," Bill agreed enthusiastically. It would certainly be more fun than whatever he was doing in his garden before his friend called, "When?"

"Thursday or Friday I would think. I still don't know exactly where it is yet?"

"I'll speak to Pat but I'll try to get a few days to give it a good look over with you. If you buy it of course, Bri?"

"Magic, Bill. If you can. I may have to move it too."

"No problem, Bri. OK, I have to run. I was just cutting the lawn and the bleedin' mower just packed up."

Brian ended the call to his Essex friend and returned to the tiled veranda to finish his coffee. His new apartment, halfway up the surrounding slopes, offered views of the avocado green canopy of the pine trees and the compact marina that opened out to the Mediterranean. He used to watch the fishing boats heading out to sea in the early morning and the cafés and bars slowly opening for business, one by one. He enjoyed his mornings overlooking his latest new home, Cassis. A tangerine and chocolate striped canopy that extended out level with the horizontal balustrade gave generous shade against the morning glare. A highly experienced traveller, he had packed the previous evening and his case sat expectantly by the front door. On top, held in place by the handle, was his flight ticket and passport. Anne had insisted she would drive Brian to Marseille airport but she had been at a family lunch and arrived somewhat inebriated. So much so that Brian didn't utter a word during the hour-long drive to catch his flight; he had little chance anyway. Anne drove his car at an average of 160kph along the highway and spoke at roughly the same speed. He wasn't known for exhibiting nerves in public, but now all a terrified Brian could do was grip either side of the base of his seat and anxiously extend his chin against his discomfort.

He arrived early to view the boat. His drive to Newhaven port, ten kilometres east of the cosmopolitan town of Brighton, was hampered by a thick coastal fog. The shallow white cliffs and the abandoned fort by the harbour entrance were hidden from view on that windless morning. Deep in the bowels of the harbour, just off the main channel out to sea was the marina for smaller pleasure craft. The fog was draped in the atmosphere like heavy, swollen spores of water. A horn blasted periodically, giving audible eyes to blind mariners. Colonies of loudly spoken gulls gathered at the end of the floating walkways, which were fixed around a pile extending above the waterline to accommodate the twice daily tide. The windless morning allowed for saline smells of boat diesel and rotten fish to stagnate in the air. Next to what appeared to be a working fishing boat, *Highroller* was draped with condensation, laid down overnight by the mist. Cylindrical buoys hung like curing sausages at regular intervals off the railing that enclosed the open section of the bow and along both sides. The name *Highroller* was sign-written on the hull. The windscreen of the cockpit rose above the roofline of the cabin at the stern and an indigo tailored awning fully enclosed the entertaining area.

"Christ, that fog is thick, *innit* Bri? I left home early this morning too. I've driven at 30mph for the last hour!" Bill had just arrived, and while walking toward Brian to embrace his friend, he provided a summary of his journey from Essex to the south coast. "I guess you won't be taking it out today?"

"Hi Bill. Nice to see you again. Thanks for coming to help. How's work going?"

"Yeah, good. The plant is due for an expansion and I'm due a promotion next year. How's the North Sea treating you?"

"I'm in my last year now. Getting a bit fed up with it."

"But still paying well, Bri?" Bill emphasised his point by nodding toward the boat Brian was planning to buy.

"Yeah, I can't complain about that. Did Pat mind you coming, Bill?"

"No, she's good as gold. It's the school holidays so she's out with the kids and your sister today."

"Oh, I saw Colleen and the kids yesterday. I flew over the day I phoned you."

"Did you see your Mum?"

"Yeah, I stayed there last night."

"How's she doing now?"

"Yeah she is a tough old bird. She had the stuffing knocked out of her when my Dad passed away, but she is getting there again. Seemed much more like herself when I saw her yesterday."

"How long ago was that, Bri?"

"My dad?" Bill nodded agreement and let Brian answer.

"Three years last month."

"Time flies, eh. Christ!" Bill then turned to look at *Highroller*. "Is this it then, Bri?"

"Yep. Not bad, eh?"

"It's bigger than I expected. But really nice though. I guess you won't be taking it out today in this weather?"

"Wouldn't have thought so, but it might clear up. We can still give it a once over."

"Beautiful boat." Bill said, envisaging how much fun his friend would be having. "Can't be cheap?"

"No, well that's my bloody problem, you see. Everything I like is either expensive, fattening or illegal!"

Highroller was moored stern in with a brace of davits for lifting and stowing a tender out of the water, above the swimming deck. They climbed aboard and gingerly moved along either bulwark while wiping the film of moisture from the cabin windows to peer inside. It quickly became apparent that a lot of work was needed to convert it into the floating gin palace that Brian was envisaging. There were no curtains for the berths, the walnut finished galley and dinette were bare without cushions and there was a toilet without a door. Its current owner clearly had a far more rudimentary approach to comfort. A separate v-berth in the bow became a double bed, with the addition of a v-shaped infill section.

"Needs a bit of work inside, Bri. And without a door on the toilet, you'll be doing your business in public!" Bill gave this humorous assessment of the river cruiser as he dried his hands on his trousers, raising a smile on Brian.

"It's not the most comfortable, I'll give you that." This came from a voice from the jetty – they both turned to see a large, turkey-breasted man with mousey eyes and salty, unkempt hair. Beads of moisture had collected over the surface of his head. They hadn't heard him arrive. Or seen him rolling his eyes dismissively at the visit from another couple of playboy landlubbers with more money than sense. Especially the one who looked like Burt Reynolds. "I'm the owner. Is one of you Brian?"

"Yep, here I am," Brian replied, almost back on the jetty and extending a hand in greeting. "Pleased to meet you."

"Terry. Terry Hayward. How do?"

As they were shaking hands, Bill reached the jetty behind Brian, "Brian Worley. And this is Bill, a good friend of mine."

"How do, Bill?"

"What do you do for a living, Brian?" Terry asked, unsure if he had more timewasters on his fishy hands.

"I'm a commercial diver, Terry. In the North Sea. And Bill is a Safety Officer at an oil refinery in Corringham in Essex."

"Ah, alright boys. I kept this for weekends, you know. Just for pleasure. With friends and family." He pointed at the neighbouring fishing boat, "but that's my everyday vehicle."

"You're a fisherman?"

"Yeah, cod and whiting mostly."

"Why are you selling it, Terry? If you don't mind me asking?"

"Business isn't so great recently and if I keep losing nets like I seem to keep doing, the house could be next!" Brian raised his dark eyebrows and extended his chin forward. "Are you planning to keep her here, 'cos the mooring is up for sale too?"

"No, only for a couple of months to fix her up then she'll be going to Marseille. I have to go back to work before I'll be able to finish."

"You live out there Brian?"

"Yeah, I do. It's magic."

"And a diver, you say? Well maybe we can have a deal on this deal, then?"

Brian liked the word 'deal' very much, but Terry would have to elaborate, "you'll have to explain Terry?"

"Well, you're a diver and I lost a net again yesterday. It's snagged on a wreck, we think."

"OK?" Brian lengthened the second syllable in curiosity.

"When the weather clears up, we can take her out for a test drive, so to speak. And you can dive down and clear my net. We have buoyed it and...."

Brian had heard enough and held out his hand in agreement to shake on it. "Deal!"

"Any repair will be cheaper than buying another fucking net."

"I'll need to organise a suit and a couple of tanks. All my gear is in France at the moment."

"I'll be able to help you out, Brian. I know a guy who goes diving with the local scuba club. He's up the yacht club regular, like. There are so many wrecks down there."

"Yeah, you can't see fucking anything but in terms of history, divers say 'the Med is dead' in comparison."

"Wish it was a bit more dead 'round here," Terry joked.

"Do you know how deep it is? Like, where you left the net?"

Terry pondered Brian's questions, rifling through a lifetime spent out at sea: "Ohh, around there. The sonar reads about a hundred and twenty feet around there, if memory serves."

"OK, that's not too deep to work using a tank. Can me and Bill work on the boat in the meantime?"

"That's fine with me. The mooring is paid yearly so you've got until May next year."

"Thanks, Terry. You say you lose a lot of nets?"

"Yeah, it always happens this time of year. The storms come rolling in after the summer, the seabed gets proper scrubbed and new things appear proud of the surface to snag us fishermen's nets."

"Do you know the name of the wreck?"

"Like I say, there a lot down there. But yeah, we think we know."

"What's it called?"

"The *Dalhousie*."

08. The *Dalhousie*

Constructed of Indian teak in Moulmein in Burma and launched in 1848, the *Dalhousie* was a first class passenger vessel named after a former Governor General of India, The Earl of Dalhousie. It was a three-masted frigate with smooth dark sides, emphasized by a continuous white stripe through which ran a solitary line of hatch windows that provided light and ventilation to the lower decks. Measuring some sixty metres in length, seven across its beam with a dry weight of 754 tons, it had been completing the passage between Plymouth and Australia on behalf of the White Horse Passenger Line. The shipping company logo of a galloping albino stallion set on a black pennant, flickered above the stern, just below the ensign flag which displayed the citizenry. Vessels such as the *Dalhousie* were the engines of Victorian wealth and power. A crew of forty-six, predominantly Indian Lascar sailors and twelve paid passengers faced a voyage of two to three months. The Indian sailors wore knee-length blue embodied tunics, white trousers and brimless, rounded Topi hats. The new ship's doctor was the last to board, a fateful commission only accepted three days prior to the voyage.

Those passengers able to afford first class passage were permitted to furnish a cabin to their expected needs and store livestock on deck, for consumption during the journey. Those of lesser means would pay for a steerage berth among the impersonal and cramped hold, level with or below the waterline of the ship. In the space not occupied by cargo, the ship supplies or galley, a long table run down the remaining length of the ship. Built against the opposing side of the hull were wooden bunks.

In bad weather or during the hours of darkness, with the windows and deck hatches sealed, the stagnant air was heavy with the vinegar used to disinfect the floors and lime powder to remove the odours.

These conditions and the long distances across the seas created fertile ground for the spread of conditions such as whooping cough or measles. The passengers travelled with all their worldly wealth, high on hope and anticipation of a new life. Packages and bundles, cases and chests, bags and boxes – even a favourite plant taken from their garden, destined for the soil of the new world.

The *Dalhousie* cleared the London docks of Blackwall on 12th October 1853: picture a scene of supplies being loaded family portrait photographs and tearful farewells from families gathered to wave off their relatives to the new life. She cast off to a fevered display of handkerchief waving and all top-hats tipped. On that crisp morning, the *Dalhousie* was towed down the Thames by a steam tug to a sheltered anchorage named 'The Downs' just off the coast of Deal, where the pilot disembarked. Contrary winter winds from the southwest detained her there for the following five nights, partially sheltered from a tossing, heavy sea. The ship's coarse rigging was forever creaking and whistling as the swirling wind passed through. Then, under the command of Captain John Butterworth, the *Dalhousie* rode out the gales with ease, fixed on a single anchor and chain throughout.

Forty-five years of age, Captain Butterworth was ever present on the quarter deck of his well-maintained ship. His bushy eyebrows and voluminous silvery beard matched the shiny jacket buttons of his otherwise weathered black uniform. His wife and two young sons had set sail from London with him, bound for Plymouth, where a further seven passengers were due to embark.

Captain Butterworth was an experienced navigator, having served for many years in the service of the ship's owner. Unaccustomed to life at sea as they were, his passengers were reassured as he overcame the uncooperative conditions with quiet confidence along with his well-tuned and obedient crew. Less scrupulous captains than Butterworth would gladly accept paying passengers, whether they had supplies to last the entire transit or not. All of the passengers on the *Dalhousie* were vetted to attest to their good health and chances of proving a burden to the colony. For most, if not all, it was their first time on a ship. Added to their visceral fear of shipwreck was an inability to swim and survive such a circumstance. Their only previous experience of wind was holding down their hats.

On the morning of the 18th October with a helpful shift in wind direction from the north west, Captain Butterworth pulled in the anchor and finally headed down the English Channel. Before them lay emigration as free settlers in a new country on the cusp of a gold rush. Tracing the long established clipper routes across the treacherous Southern Ocean, the only port due after Plymouth would be Cape Town at the southern tip of Africa. From there, Captain Butterworth would have to calculate his route. The further south he dared steer the *Dalhousie* into the southern Indian Ocean, the stronger the winds and faster the route. But this also brought the risk of huge waves, unbroken by any land mass, and icebergs. Depending on the season, the target was the 'Roaring Forties', fierce winds that blew east-to-west through a circumpolar corridor between forty and fifty degrees south of the equator. But the *Dalhousie* wouldn't even reach Plymouth in Devon, or round the Cape of Good Hope, let alone Australia. Within twenty-four hours, it would lay foundered at the bottom of the English Channel.

By ten o'clock that morning the wind carried the ship past the point of Dungeness, ten miles off the starboard beam. Much to Captain Butterworth's disappointment, the fickle wind weakened, so he continued to navigate the channel under full sail, labouring at half the speed they had achieved earlier in the morning.

"Batten down the hatches," cried Captain Butterworth to his crew. He could feel the wind changing once again, and for the worse. "Reef the top sails!" came the following strained command.

Long after sunset, while the waxing moon was concealed above a raw, clouded sky, the open deck operated in gaslight. The lighthouse at Beachy Head was just in sight off the starboard side, at a distance estimated to be between six to eight miles. The ship's hold was all but dark, the steerage passengers were unsighted, and some were vomiting from the increasingly turbulent motion of the ship. Barrels were rolling around, getting bumped and thumped against beams, pitched and tossed against crude deal boards, not a single surface of which was planed. Blowing a gale from the south east and tormented by a heavy swell, the *Dalhousie* was now facing its fate on a furious stretch of sea.

By four o'clock the next morning, all of the sails apart from the main sail were double tied and the anchor had been dropped just as the *Dalhousie* lurched deeply on her starboard side, an angle acute enough to suggest it wouldn't recover.

All the passengers and crew felt the anchor give way shortly after as the *Dalhousie* rolled over on her port side flanks. Rich or poor, paid passenger or seamen, they were all the same now. The first wave that hit carried the long boat away – the pigs and goats that had been housed inside it were thrown in the churning sea. Captain Butterworth sensed the ship was no longer watertight and gave the order while braced against the ships wheel, "Haul to the wind. Jettison the water tanks, the timber and the sheep pens!" It was his one shot at rebalancing his ship that he suspected was already laden with water.

As the waves grew in scale, occasionally breaking over the deck, the tanks, lumber and livestock were tossed overboard. The sheep's bleating only lasted a few seconds before they were overwhelmed. Every soul onboard the stricken *Dalhousie* was at the mercy of the wind, the waves and the pendulum effect of a flooded hull. An angry swell then passed under the hull, rolling the liquid ballast back across the hold. A final keel onto her starboard side brought the masthead down into the waves, where it would remain. With the loss of the main sail, carried away along with the main mast when it was sheared, they were doomed. The *Dalhousie* was settling fast in the water, prone on her starboard side with the pounding waves washing over her. For every extra cubic metre of water in the hull, the ship took on another ton in weight. Great gargles and rushes of air were heard below deck as the icy waters rose inside her, forcing the deck hatches to burst open. The petrified passengers were hauled out onto a deck that was near perpendicular and faced their fate dressed only in their night dress. The rain and spray generated by the waves breaking over the hull were indistinguishable from each other and did little to abate their terror. But the rain tasted sweet in the mouth against the bitter saltiness of the spray.

"Do what you can to save yourselves!" Captain Butterworth shouted. Still attempting to assume control of a panicked flight for survival, he told whoever was still alive on or in the water around the *Dalhousie* to head for a schooner that was bearing down on the wreck, having been sighted some half a mile away. One couple sat serenely in prayer with their two children on the capsized hull, resigned to their fate before a final wave broke over them. The last remaining chance at survival for some, the quarter boat, was afloat behind the mizzen mast. Captain Butterworth desperately ordered four Lascars to hold the boat in place while his wife and children were allowed to climb into it. But in the utter confusion of the moment, the Lascars panicked and the quarter boat drifted off into the furious night, with some encased ship documents but all of its life-preserving berths empty.

At 5:30am, only ten minutes after the main mast was lost and the ship was no longer buoyant, the *Dalhousie* sank nose first. Sailors on the nearby schooner shouted for survivors to swim to her, but did nothing to lessen their speed by pulling in the sails. Combined with the strength of the tide this made it an impossible request. Some survivors floated on pieces of wreckage but by sunrise, only two hours later, all but one was drowned or had yielded to hypothermia. Within a day, the bodies were washed up below the cliffs of Beachy Head. The wreckage would be collected in Hastings and Rye Bay. The first victim to be found and identified was Mrs. Butterworth, the wife of the late commander of the *Dalhousie*. She was discovered by a fisherman just off the Hastings coast. He had been drawn to an object in the water, and found a body wearing nothing but a chemise, nightgown, two petticoats, stockings and boots.

09. Finger Trouble

Brian's strategic delays with courses earned him a near three-month sojourn in the south of France. It was time well spent in the bosom of Budda Hermitage, his adopted French family. Anne's mother, Claudia, an elegant lady of considerable breeding, adored her English gentleman guest, who was only ever polite, erudite, charming and always welcome. Anne's two brothers and numerous visiting guests basked in Brian's subsea tales. Maximilian enjoyed all the theatre associated with using Brian and his Maserati as a taxi service to or from his office in the centre of Marseille. In his daughter's estimation, Brian and her father were a well-matched pair of posing rogues, just very lovable ones.

But his delayed return to *Smit Lloyd 112* had knocked him out of sync with Geoff's shift. After three months of continuous, unrelenting French sun, Aberdeen's drizzle and the gales that complicated his helicopter landing on the vessel were a bad starting point to his return. Wearing his red hard hat and carrying Brian's, both labelled with similar embossed tape, Geoff left the relative civility of the cabin to greet his friend. Under the wash of the helicopter blades that were slowing with each rotation, Geoff had some bad news for Brian in an informal handover.

"I'm leaving, Bri. This was my last hitch out here. I got a contract in Brazil."

"Oh, bollocks. I was just in the office, nobody told me. You're not pulling my leg?"

"No, Bri. It's with Marsat. Gonna be based in Rio. I'm starting in the new year so I'm going to have a few months off now, just like you."

"Bollocks," Looking for more positive news about the forthcoming four weeks on the *112*, Brian asked about their new partner.

"And how is young Mickey getting on?"

"I guess they didn't tell you about Mickey in the office either?" Geoff then answered his own rhetorical sounding question. "He's dead."

Brian's eyes closed momentarily as he winced, "How? Fuck. What happened? At work, yeah?" Brian asked, not awaiting the answer with greatest anticipation.

"Well between you and me, the word is he was fed some bad gas and it's been covered up. I was bellman so it didn't affect me. Did have a funny smell in there just before we think it happened. We were kept in the pot at depth so I don't know for sure. But the police and safety officers came aboard and we stopped operations for a few days. They switched the air supply to a new cylinder and Kaare just shrugged his shoulders. He's claiming diver fatigue this time I think."

"You recovered Mickey?"

"I had to."

"When?"

"My hitch before this. Five or six days in sat by that time. Not cool, eh?"

"So who you been working with?"

"I got another Frenchie who couldn't speak English now. I hear you have two new guys working with you."

"Not that pair of pillocks on my flight out here I hope?" One look into their cabin confirmed his worst fears. "Where's that fucking Operations Manager. Fucking Pierre?"

"Hang on, I haven't finished with the good news. You'll be using a Mobile Diving Unit."

"What the fuck is that?"

"M.D.U? It's basically a normal bell that's self-propelled. The pilot capsule is at normal pressure mounted on top of it. They came up with it for times when we have a worksite that is too far to from the ship. They can't re-anchor the ship if we are working just beyond the length of our umbilicals."

"OK. And one of those soppy pricks is going to drive me around in that?"

"Think so, Bri"

"Does it work?"

"Not really, no. It took two hours to travel a hundred feet the last time. The winter is starting to close in already. There's been a lot of aborted dives this hitch. And now there's this stupid new contraption they are trying to make work. And you know what Kaare's like, he won't listen to anyone."

Before setting off to locate the Operations Manager, Brian handed Geoff his luggage and made a request: "Save me a seat if you can, please. I won't be long. Fuck this."

With his index finger cocked to emphasise his disapproval, Brian entered Pierre's office without knocking. Pierre was a spindly man with a coiffured perm, Hawaiian shirt and brown tinted spectacles every bit as thick as the base of a champagne bottle. An Anglo-Franco exchange of views ensued, rich in the cockney art form of excessive profanity.

"You wanna try to feed me bullshit. I ain't eating it. Fuck you!"

Pierre's black hair dye was already out of step with his complexion, but now he looked even paler. He apparently had no counter for such frankness.

"Bri-yon. What do you mean?"

"No fucking way!"

"Bri-yon, don't be like *zis*."

"Not a fucking chance. I was in the office before I got the chopper and this job is fuck all like what they told me."

"Br...."

Brian cut him off before another appeal. "You've got me with two piss-pot amateurs, OK. You know I refuse to work only with rookies. And I'll never let one check my gear either, thank you very fucking much. Secondly, they ain't even experienced. I've seen one of them already. The fucking pussy is embroidering his fucking jeans in our cabin."

"Ah, you mean Samuel?"

"What the fuck! And now I learn that Kaare fucking killed our last novice, Mickey. I liked him, he seemed a good lad too. Mark my fucking words, that Norwegian pillock will do the same to one of them or fucking me on this trip."

Brian left Pierre in state of confusion and returned to the helideck, where the helicopter was readying to leave with the divers who had just finished their respective hitches. Brian cupped his mouth to amplify himself and shouted at the pilot through his window. "Room for one more?" The pilot pushed his forearm through the narrow opening and gave Brian a thumbs-up while flicking his head in the direction of the rear entrance.

Brian's attempted resignation had the opposite effect to what he was expecting. When he returned to the office. Rather than a wave goodbye, he was promptly given a pay increase and new working conditions were sanctioned. His request that Kaare wasn't solely responsible for the diving operations and would be overseen on each of Brian's future dives by a second person, be it Pierre or the ship's captain, was approved on the spot, as was his request to select a crew from the divers already on the *112*.

They couldn't afford to lose an experienced diver like Brian, especially so soon after Geoff. Man-sized loopholes in the tax breaks for commercial divers were being closed. Add to this unionization of the industry and the fact that many experienced divers were taking flight to oil fields around the world. Common sense dictates that if the less experience your divers have, the more it increases the likelihood of accidents. Add to this all the negative publicity such events would generate and their unease at letting Brian resign as he intended was understandable.

With an increased salary, he approached the same helicopter for a third time that day. The pilot was shaking his head in confusion as Brain pointed to the grey sky and spoke through a grin, "Taxi!"

"I wish you'd make your bloody mind up," came the reply.

The aborted dives all added up to lost man hours on the seabed and both Kaare and the captain, Hurricane Jim, were under increasing pressure to commence operations as soon as possible. The conditions didn't concern Hurricane Jim – he had earned his nickname, when stationed in the Gulf of Mexico, as the last skipper to return to shore when a hurricane was in the area. The recent conditions that Geoff had warned of persisted after Brian's return to the *112*. His first scheduled dive was abandoned long before any thought was given to suiting up. From inside the chamber, it felt calmer the following day. Kaare gave the go-ahead and Brian began to prepare with his crew of one, chosen from the 'best of the rest'. It was a simple selection process. All the requirements were; must be able to speak English, must not be a new starter and therefore had done the job before. So when compared to the company of the new recruits, a husky voiced Scotsman called Mike was suggested to and accepted by Brian. He had been working for a few months and once Brian knew he had worked with Geoff during his French sabbatical, he was sold. Mike would be bellman, in charge supplying Brian with all his air and hot water needs.

"OK, this is dive control. Are you receiving in the bell?" Kaare's pale voice crackled through the speaker in the diving bell.

Brian replied by pressing transmit button on the bell radio, "Diver one receiving. Ready to transfer."

Sat on fold-down bench seats, wedged between two coiled umbilicals, Brian could feel the support technicians removing the clamps around the housing that connected the bell to the compression chambers. The crane cable pulled tight, ready to lift them clear of the vessel and down into the depths. The bell bobbed and jerked through the swell and continued to mimic the movement of the *112* once submerged. The compensators fitted to the crane, designed to cancel out excessive movement, were having little effect. Seconds after Kaare confirmed the bell had reached its working depth, its base slammed into the seabed, as the swell on the surface was greater than the distance usually left in calmer conditions between the bell and the bottom.

"Pull the bell up!" Brian ordered, furious in the knowledge that if he had left the bell just before it struck the sea floor, he would probably be dead. "Five metres and I'll work with a longer umbilical."

"Bell lifted, Diver One."

Brian allowed a stifled "fuck" to exit his mouth before pressing the transmit button, "OK. Thanks."

Brian already had his dark red suit on and lifted his helmet over his head while Mike turned the wheel to unlock the bell door. After Mike had attached Brian's umbilical, he observed Diver One squeeze himself through the bell door and then informed top side, "Diver One in the water."

Diver One had to oversee the adjustment of a squared five-ton rock, which was no longer acting as solid ballast after shifting during a recent storm. Following that he had open a valve on a well-head manifold, for which Geoff had replaced the faulty pump during his last hitch.

Both Geoff's attempts to complete the tasks had been curtailed as each dive thereafter had been aborted.

"OK, thank you Bellman. Diver One, if all systems are good, we will start with moving the ballast stone. Please confirm when you are in position and ready to finish fitting the lifting straps?"

"OK, topside. Will do. Can we also confirm that Jim is on the same frequency?"

"Hi Brian, sorry Diver One I meant, pal. Jim is hearing you loud and clear."

"OK, proceeding toward work site. Visibility bad. Must be down to two feet," Brian reported. "OK, Diver One ready to fit the lifting straps." He was always mindful not to chunter to himself as the microphone in his helmet broadcast everything into Kaare's headphones on the surface.

"OK, Diver One."

"One looks like it's in place and connected to the rig crane. The second still needs running around properly. I'll get on with that. Please lift the slack on the first strap so it clears out of my way."

"OK, Diver One." Kaare communicated with the rig to lightly lift the crane until it bit, reiterating that they should be careful as he had a man in the water, eighty metres below. The boulder rolled on its axis, budged towards Brian and then suddenly rolled over his right hand. For a second or two, before the weight lifted, his hand was pinned between a squared slab of granite and the foot of the pipeline support.

"AAAAAAAAAAAAAAHHHHHHHHHHHHHHHH.....HOLY FUUUUUCCCCCCCCKKKKK!" Before Kaare had time to ask what the problem was, Diver One alerted the surface. "LIFT, LIFT, LIFT. FFFFFFFUUUUUCCCCKKKKKK!"

Three fingers and thumb on Brian's right hand were crushed beneath the ballast rock as it shifted when lifted by the crane, compacting his carpels. When it was freed seconds later, he instinctively brought what remained of his palm up toward the glass window in his helmet. Even in cloudy water, his hand was clearly a tangled mess of flesh, white bone and skin. Losing a finger or fingers was occupational hazard, many of Brian's colleagues were minus at least one digit and it looked like he had just joined the club. An advantage of the icy waters was it would numb exposed body parts within seconds, so Brian removed his shredded glove.

"Diver One, return to the bell. Dive aborted. You're working time is nearly up too," came Kaare's caring response. "Bellman, prepare the bell for a return to the surface."

"Fuck you, topside. The Bellman can't swap with me 'cos if he has a problem, I can't rescue him. The way I fucking see it is we are stuck we each other. Ahhhhhhhh, and I've just tied the bell off so you can't lift it. I still have another job to do and I've more chance of doing it than those bozos up in the chamber. Even with one fucking hand!"

"Diver One, if you don't return to the bell now you'll be fired."

Jim cut in to defend the injured Diver One, "Brian, Kaare may have just fired you, but if you get that valve working on the wellhead manifold, I'm sure there will be a bonus in it for you! A big one!"

From that moment, Kaare was helpless in his control room. He was impotent against the will of Diver One and would view it as a mutiny. The Dive Supervisor now a passenger on his own operation. Ironically, having been dismissed on the grounds of not following safety procedure, Brian's sacking had little impact on the remainder of his career in the North Sea as it was seen out in a hospital bed in Stavanger, Norway.

10. Rhône

Terry's reservations about the boating credentials of the pair that had bought his boat were confirmed soon after *Highroller* made its delayed exit from Newhaven marina, bound for France. Within an hour, Brian had made his first navigation error. After hugging the south coast for longer than he should have done and supposedly maintaining an ESE bearing towards Calais, Bill made a suggestion to Captain Worley. Sitting, appropriately enough, in the navigator's chair, Bill was corroborating the features of the coast on the horizon with the map and compass.

"Bri, I reckon you have to turn right!"

"Eh?" Brian replied.

"You're heading towards Norway at the moment, Bri!"

Brian's jaw extended below a naughty smile as he pulled *Highroller* right. The navigator continued to issue advice to his disorientated skipper: "Now, just stay on a south east course now and we should end up somewhere near Calais. Then we'll follow the coast to Le Havre where we get into the canals. Yeah?"

"Roger," agreed Captain Worley, sagely.

Thankfully, Bill had been invited along to help on the passage along with Carol, a 22-year-old student who worked in the Comex office in Aberdeen in her spare time. Her main attribute was her willingness to leap off the boat to secure a mooring and manage the opening of the locks. Add to this her French linguistic skills and she made a fine addition to the crew. Unfortunately, her predilection for listening to her Abba cassettes hadn't been taken into consideration, prior to the voyage. *Highroller* had been kitted out with tailored cushions, upholstered in white leatherette. In the cabin, a dinette and galley which converted into two berths and the v-berth in the bow, had privacy curtains fitted on tracks that ran above and below each window. Brian was pleased he had been able to invite Bill along, as it was small payback for all the hours over the winter Bill had helped fix up *Highroller*. Bill had benefited from this as he was planning on buying a boat of his own. But Brian couldn't have done this journey on his own. His hand had healed somewhat since his accident and the surgeon had managed to save all his fingers. The knuckle in his index finger had to be fused together with screws. But he was a long way from regaining full range of motion and the scarring was still tight and proud. His finger was medially crooked and a quarter of an inch shorter than when he had last given the peace sign.

Passing by the white cliffs and pebble beaches of Northern France, Bill was proved correct and they reached Le Havre in the early afternoon. The pointed steeple of St Joseph's church overlooked the town, the huge container port and the mouth of the Seine River. It was intended to be a pleasure cruise and had felt a little too much like hard work thus far, so they decided to find a mooring for the night on the Seine once they were through the first lock. The lock gates sat welcomingly ajar as Captain Worley gently brought *Highroller* into the chamber that would raise to the level beyond the exit gates. Carol had already leapt overboard and stood dripping while on standby to close the entrance gates.

Bill had moved to the tapered point of the bow, ready to toss Carol a line if it were necessary.

Following their graceful arrival into lock number one, Bill braced himself for a gentle bump against the exit gates. However, Brian had slightly misjudged the controlled drift into the filling chamber and needed to check the momentum. Already idling the engines in neutral, Captain Worley pulled back on the two throttle arms. *Highroller* lurched backwards far more quickly that Bill had expected and, accompanied by the sound of two bare feet sliding on wet fiberglass, he silkily disappeared over the bow.

"Bri!"

Captain Worley didn't see *Highroller*'s Navigator enter the water, but he heard the splash and saw the resulting concentric circles widening across the surface of the lock which confirmed it. Although he hoped his friend was OK, his body was consumed in a convulsive laughter fit that hindered his breathing and wet his eyes as he was forced to desert the bridge. Carol's loud cackle at the same incident did little to calm Captain Worley's amusement down. Bill's inelegant arrival on the swimming deck, with his white t-shirt stained spinach green by the abundance of algae in the lock, re-ignited the giggles just when had they began to subside.

"Blood-dy hell, Bri!" said Bill, who was starting to get the joke himself. Once he was capable of speech, Brian blamed his misjudgment on his injured hand.

Ahead of them lay 800 miles and three weeks of milky blue rivers and canals. There would be in excess of two hundred locks, so they would have ample time to practice the procedure that had gone so awry during the first attempt. The route would lead through Paris and then dead south through Lyon to Marseille on the Rhône river. They were traveling along cuttings, diversion canals, aqueducts, embankments, through tunnels and under stone bridges so low they had to duck. They were offered views of the ruined chateaus, ancient roman towns, sloping vineyards and lavender fields. Supple willow trees crowded the river's edge and softly reflected in the polished current.

Each day, Carol took flight from their mooring on a fold-up bike. Armed with her schoolgirl French, she would return with wine, cheese, a baguette and the ingredients for another bloody cassoulet. One errand beyond her known French was to track down a grease nipple. *Highroller* had suffered a broken prop shaft and Brian needed a new tip for his grease gun.

"My schoolgirl French doesn't extend to 'a nipple for a grease gun', Brian. Think you'll have to come with me."

As daunting a lingual undertaking as it may have seemed, imagine the confusion of the hardware store owner. There you were behind your counter when in walked a Burt Reynolds lookalike and what appeared to be his fair-haired daughter. They said something unintelligible in English before Burt formed both hands together as if holding an invisible handgun, complete with his crooked index finger pulling an imaginary trigger. Your absolute non-comprehension of their requirements only seemed to spur them on. Undaunted, your customer then lifted up his white t-shirt to expose his hairless chest before he repeatedly points at his left nipple while saying something else in English. The daughter then started giggling and pulling her father's t-shirt down before they decided to leave your shop empty-handed, almost completely helpless with laughter. Thankfully, one engine was enough to get *Highroller* to the next boatyard where Brian could take his grease gun into the various workshops and point at the part he needed, rather than a body part.

Each day of the trip south proved more beautiful than the last: the early morning cups of tea under the awning of the cockpit while the breaking sun rid the river of its surface mist, forever disturbed by fish jumping above the water, evading larger predator species; the undulating landscape dotted with oat coloured stone buildings with blood red tiled roofs; and the daily lottery of ingredients Carol would return with for lazy lunches after her morning cycle to the nearest village.

Around the table on the open deck behind the cockpit, they sat eating cheese, tearing at a baguette and chewing slices of dried meat. At the request of the sunburnt crew, Brian anchored in a shaded meander on the Rhône and folded the awning down. Amid the sounds of cutlery clinking on plates and wine or cognac glasses undergoing constant re-fueling and the musical offerings of Abba, talk turned to Brian's future. His clingy t-shirt and black trunks were slowly drying after his time spent in the water fixing the shear pin. As he spoke he alternated fiddling with a hammer and a screwdriver on the table, the tools he had used to finish his repair.

"Well, I'm done now. In the North Sea I mean."

"So what now, Bri. You've got that bonus still?" Bill asked.

"Yeah. That's in the bank in Jersey. I'm thinking of starting my own company."

"Still with diving?"

"Yeah, more salvage than operations though."

"Shipwrecks, Bri?"

"Any interesting ones, Brian?" Carol asked.

"Not really, Carol. Me and a few guys used to pillage here and there up and down the east coast of Scotland in our off time. But we never really found anything. A few cannons, that kind of thing. No gold."

"Must be strange, diving on a wreck were people died. Spooky, like diving on a grave or something?"

Brian smiled and answered Carol: "No, there isn't anything like that left, normally. Just lumps and bumps on the seabed and a few exposed parts of the ship."

"Must be interesting though, Bri?"

"Yeah it is. I'm pretty tired of working offshore now though. I sold up all my stuff in Arbroath when I got back there from Norway. I've worked out there for nearly three years now. The real money is in being a middle man, you know. Providing divers and taking a share of the profits."

"In between who, Bri?"

"Marine surveyors. Prospectors. Investors. Governments. Whoever wants to hire me, I guess." The diving community was close knit and everyone seemed to know each other or of each other. More and more opportunities were out there for those crazy enough to breathe helium mix gas through an umbilical at a depth of hundred metres deep or more to retrieve precious cargo. Advances in technology had enabled a rush to salvage wrecks previously unreachable in oceans and seas and lakes and fjords. The equipment used to detect the treasure was improving and accessibility was improving at the same pace. Diving provided Brian with the platform to explore other options and the crazier the plan, the harder Brian found it to refuse. But one and all of these future deals would need collateral. "I've had contact with a guy I know who is working on a salvage job in Mauritania."

"Blood-dy hell, Bri. That's west Africa, innit?"

"Yeah, just below Morocco. And I've been chatting to a guy in Paris called Omer about another deal in Morocco. There are a load of wrecks around the coast of Morocco from Operation Torch during World War Two. It was before the D-Day landings, when the Yanks teamed up with us Brits against the French navy."

"Christ, I didn't know about that, Bri."

"Yeah, not a lot of people know that one. And I know where they are!" Brian said with a knowing grin. "But we'll see how that works. There's talk of a production company wanting to make a documentary about it too."

"What was the story you told me last time? About the gold, Bri," Bill already remembered most of the story, but Carol probably hadn't heard it.

"With the two ex-SAS guys?"

"Yeah. Christ, Bri. Wait until you here this Carol!"

The lunch had extended over the afternoon and Brian had consumed sufficient cognac to talk freely about his life of deals and agreements. "I got contacted by these two ex-SAS guys who wanted to salvage gold that had been ditched by Indian traders who were smuggling it into Morocco."

"Why were they ditching it, Brian?"

"Apparently, they were known to ditch anything illegal if the Berber Guards patrolling the ports wanted to come aboard for an inspection. They reckon the site was just over the border, in Algerian waters. The two SAS guys had this salvage barge with bloody machine guns fixed on each end. But when we were just about to head out to sea, the Moroccan authorities bottled it and pulled the plug."

"You're a boy, Bri!" Bill yawned. All the daytime wine had made them drowsy.

"I'll have to turn in soon, guys. I'm cream crackered." Bill's yawning had proved contagious.

Without the relative comforts of home, the days were devoted to keeping *Highroller* moving toward the Mediterranean and the evenings were spent cooking and consuming yet another cassoulet. They grew increasingly in tune with the sun, waking at sunrise for breakfast and being back in bed as it sunk over the horizon. They followed the river for another five days before they arrived in Marseille, to a great welcome from Anne and her family at Budda Hermitage. After those two hundred locks, all of their hands were dry, cracked and blistered. And if they never saw another cassoulet again, that would be a bonus.

11. Cabo Frio

Carol and Bill both returned to the UK: Bill back to his family life and onto the oil refinery, and Carol back to her studies and her part-time hours in the Comex office in Aberdeen. Although not before Maximilian had taught Carol how to correctly fire a Derringer pistol in the basement firing range. The tutorial followed Carol's first shots that were all fired into the ceiling. Brian had managed to secure a berth in Cassis harbour and could see *Highroller* from his veranda. He was otherwise occupied with setting up his company – Salvamar. The name had come up in conversations with Maximilian, during the drive to or from his office in Marseille, and long boozy lunches and evening dinners of many courses in the grounds of Budda Hermitage.

The word alluded to the two key elements of the business, salvage and marine, and coincidentally it was the Romanian word for 'Lifeguard'. Anne was helping Brian with the translation involved with setting a business up in a country where he didn't speak the language. There was also an issue converting the Franc to Pounds or Dollars. At one point Brian and Anne visited a new development that was under construction on an island just offshore from Marseille: a marina-based office development with combined living quarters. During the viewing of a show example, Brian misplaced a zero in his financial conversion, prompting his announcement to the estate agent that he could afford two and would therefore be interested in buying a pair of neighbouring units. The agent's eyes flickered with commission on

SALVAMAR – A TALE OF SALVAGE & DEEP DIVING

hearing this. Brian's eyes also flickered when back in Marseille, Anne explained the true cost of just a single apartment, let alone two.

With the newspaper spread out on a table overlooking Cassis marina, he scanned through the adverts for business premises Anne had circled for him. But he had no idea what was written so resigned himself to drink another beverage and wait for Anne to arrive on her mini motorbike. While he was confusing himself further operating his chromed coffee machine in the kitchen, the phone rang. Brian folded his legs under himself as he sat down on the end of the sofa closest to the phone, just inside the veranda doors.

"Hello? Battersea Dogs Home?" Brian said in jest, certain if the caller was French it was a joke purely for his own enjoyment.

"Hello, Is that Brian?" Geoff asked, down a crackly line.

"Ahh, hello Geoff. Nice to hear from you. Yeah you're talking to Brian."

"How you doing, old man?"

"I'm good. Just moved the boat down to Marseille. You're lucky you caught me. Only got back a few days ago."

"How's the hand doing? I heard about the accident."

Brian held his hand up in front of his face while he gave Geoff a progress report. "I've still got all my fingers. Had a few operations in Norway, mind. Bit of a crooked finger. My doctor said I'll never play the piano again though!".

"Silly arse. Are you busy at the moment, Bri?"

"Not really. A few irons in the fire, you know me. Why?"

"Good. Because we need you in Brazil, Bri. If you're keen?"

"Yeah, I'd be keen but aren't I too old now though? I'm over forty?"

"Don't worry about that. You can be as old or young as you want to be here."

"Are you saying what I think you are saying, Geoff?"

"Yeah, we can sort your papers out. How much younger would you like to be, Bri? Five years?"

"That'll do. Magic!"

"I'll be in touch, Bri. I'll get someone from the office to send you a telex and you can get a flight booked. Leave it with me."

Brian replaced the receiver after Geoff had put his end down. He pulled his brows down and pushed his jaw out while he contemplated the sudden development in his future. In his head, he was finished and done with oilfield diving. It was an industry under evolution and with constant technological advancements, Remotely Operated Vehicles, (ROV's) were taking more and more tasks out of the hands of divers. Initially brought into service as an observational eye over the divers for surface-based dive supervisors, ROV's were now taking still and real-time video footage of underwater structures. Designs of wellhead manifolds, pumps and valves were increasingly including ROV operation within their scope. It was a benefit in terms of health and safety for the divers but a hindrance in terms of the collective wallets of the industry.

Geoff's offer, although very welcome and attractive, was also somewhat inconvenient with regard to getting Salvamar off the ground. There were deals to finance though, and the work in Brazil would assist with that, as well as opportunities in Morocco and Mauritania to pursue. Brian still had the bonus from his last dive in the North Sea, but if the deals worked out as he hoped, the pay-out would be swiftly swallowed up before there was any prospect of payback. His only immediate plans were to fully procrastinate on *Highroller* in Cassis while preparing to move her down to Gibraltar. To devote the next weeks to drinking cognac on the rear deck or find himself hypnotised by the caustic water reflections or watching the harbour fry nibble the algae on his mooring line, all set to the gentle throng of marine engines sweeping past on tick over. But Brazil was an offer he simply couldn't refuse. Within three days, his flight to Rio de Janeiro was booked and his luggage was full again.

So, Brian would be running around the world for a few more years yet. Now back permanently in Marseille following a homeward transfer from Aberdeen, Anne agreed to help Brian out with organising things in Cassis so he could continue to pursue deals with Salvamar. Almost immediately Rio de Janeiro proved wilder than Cassis. The short bus journey from his hotel on Copacabana Beach had proven that. Three masked gunman entered at the next stop, and managed to rob anyone who resembled a tourist within another three stops. There wasn't a jot of resistance or concern from the driver: he treated the incident as routine as if they were a hop-on hop-off conductors checking for tickets. Amid the frightened screams and shocked remonstrations, Brian pulled some damp cash from his denims and claimed that was all he had. It wasn't the first time a gun had been pulled on him: his brothers-in-law in Athens had seen to that.

Brian had arrived that morning with a mere four-hour difference worth of jet lag to contend with and fitted in immediately. Everything, everyone and everywhere was offbeat enough to suit him. The continuous soundtrack of suggestive samba, flirty salsa and sassy bossanova music began as soon as the doors of the aircraft opened. It was audible through the airport terminal, in the taxi ride, and even from the submerged bar in the hotel swimming pool that lulled him off for a siesta in his room. A distinctly foreign city, built on the endless summer and year-round partying, it opened up before him on the train ride up to Christ the Redeemer, the famous soapstone figure overseeing the city, at the summit of Corcovado mountain. The Latin American sun was sinking into the Atlantic Ocean, the light was ever softening into evening and the statue Brian stood beneath slowly began to wear the lights shining upwards from its plinth. Sugarloaf Mountain was across the bay, whose waters were surrounded with yachts, reduced to white dots in the scale.

The viewing deck extended out in front of the structure, its parameters girded with buxom marble spindles supporting carved stone balustrades. The last rays of the sun shot through the spindles, casting alternate fingers of light and shade on the smooth stone floor. The hammered finish of the coin-operated telescopes was beginning to reflect the lights from the bar adjacent to the plinth. Umbrellas were spread along one side of the deck in front of the bar, each equipped with its own autonomous colony of insects, drawn to the bulbs softly illuminating each table. Brian was there to meet Charles Raynor, the Saturation Manager for Marsat, the company with a contract to provide diving services to the majority state-run oil company, PetroBras. Geoff had been coy about the description of Brian's 'date', he only provided Charles's nickname – 'The Colonel' and insisted with some amusement that Brian was smart enough to work out the rest.

The romantic time of day and setting meant there was only one solitary man stood at the bar: the rest of the clientele were paired off in couples. Charles, or the Colonel, wasn't wearing military uniform or decorated with a chest of medals. He was turned out in tan cowboy boots, blue jeans and a white shirt open to navel to display a gold medallion and a hairy, sunburnt chest. His wavy hair was slicked back and goatee beard impeccably trimmed: both were the colour of ivory. A pair of black half-brow glasses rested on his bridge-less nose. Brian was still enjoying Geoff's observant riddle as he greeted the Colonel, tempted to ask how to fry chicken.

"Hey, Brian. Great to meet you, bud," said The Colonel, the only thing louder than his Texan accent was his bad aftershave. "What are you drinking, bud?"

"Hmmm, a cognac please."

Charles filled the awkward silence by looking at a display of shucked oysters on the bar that were perched on a bed of crushed ice in large bowl. "You want some oysters, bud?"

Brian refused: he was more of a jellied eels kind of man, "No, it's OK. They aren't my favourite."

"They're delicious. I ordered a dozen when I got here earlier and I tell you bud, they were so good, I ordered another dozen! Are you sure you don't want some?"

"Yeah, I'm sure, thanks."

"No problem. Sorry to drag you all the way up here Brian, but I run an account here and bring a lot of clients."

"Not such a bad place to spend my first evening here." While he was no fan of mixing with rig bosses and diving managers when it came to work, it was another story when they were feeding him fine cognacs and lobster thermidor.

"You arrived this morning? And Geoff has been speaking to you from the ship?"

"Yeah, I got a hotel in Copacabana for a couple of days while we work everything out. Geoff mentioned there is a staff flat along the coast that I can use?"

"That's right, bud. In Cabo Frio. I'll get the keys from the office in town tomorrow, bud. Please use it until you find a place, OK?"

"Magic."

"You married, Brian?"

"Technically yes. I married a Greek girl in 1962 and my lawyer in Athens can't track her down to sign the divorce papers!"

"OK, bud. That's great."

"This place reminds me a lot of Athens, just more lush."

"It's a beautiful part of the world, bud."

"Smashing," Brian agreed. The bar lady had already given him the eye when pouring his second cognac. The dark grey hairs at his temple and sprinkled through his moustache had only added to his rugged, windswept attraction.

"What car do you drive, bud?"

"A Maserati."

"Damn! Italian iron! Which one, bud?"

"Merak. I've spent the same amount as the asking price fixing the baastard though."

"Beautiful though, bud. Eh, there is no begging for shaggin' when a Maserati is your wagon!"

"No comment."

The Colonel brought their attention onto work matters, the reason for the meeting. "Geoff recommends you very highly. You guys worked a lot in the North Sea together?"

"Yep, that's right. A few thousand hours we reckon. I like working with him and never had any incidents either. He's always got your back, you know?"

"That's great, bud. Geoff told me the same about you. Experience is a bit thin on the ground here, so you won't be working together. You'll be working with Ron. Another Brit. You know that, right?"

"No, I didn't. But that's OK. Not a problem."

"You can work as many days in saturation as you like. Even dive supervising if you feel like it. Geoff tells me you have done that before too?"

"Geoff is right again."

Brian fully intended to take advantage of the offer to work as many hours as possible, whether in saturation and supervising from the surface. The extension to his career in South America was only for five years and was dependent on him remaining alive and local officials not noticing his counterfeit papers.

"Things are a bit dodgy here, not like the North Sea. but the upside is you are 35 all over again," The Colonel raised his forever full glass in mock celebration, "So, happy birthday, Brian. And welcome to Rio."

"Cheers."

So the next chapter of Brian's dangerous profession would be under the open expanse of the southern Atlantic, the North Sea just a veritable trench in contrast – at the behest of big-buckle belt-wearing oil field 'tough' guys like Charles. Thankfully, while the divers were mostly unseen and unsung, they weren't underpaid.

12. Helicopter

Brian's new floating home was the dive support vessel, *Star Hercules*, which was anchored on the cobalt waters above the Campos Basin oilfield, some two hundred kilometres east of Rio De Janeiro. The helicopter escorting him, a bull-nosed Hughes 500, vibrated and juddered alarmingly during the hour-long flight. It was a 6-seat civilian aircraft, small in comparison to the 16-seaters flown out of Aberdeen or Stavanger, and was painted glossy black with gold lettering and company decals. Brian managed his fear by gauging the pilot, sat just in front of him, who appeared unconcerned about the aircraft's ability to reach the *Star Hercules* and return to shore with Geoff.

The new 'norms' would be greater depths, wilder colleagues and lower safety standards. His deepest dive in the North Sea could be considered shallow on the *Star Hercules*, which was floating some three hundred metres above the floor of the Southern Atlantic. The brutal heat and humidity, however uncomfortable in direct sunlight, was a welcome improvement on the bitterness of the North Sea. In the distance, dolphins broke the water's surface, iridescent under the sun. Pods of whales drifted to and fro with the occasional breach.

"OK guys, we have a change of plan for your first dive together. We have a recovery job to do first I'm afraid. A chopper put out a distress signal before dropping off the radar nearby. Something has been picked up on the sonar and the ROVs are down there at the moment. Two fatalities suspected. Start preparing, over. We are just moving the ship into position." Their new task crackled through the intercom into the compression chamber. "We will continue with the press down to the normal working depth. Oh, and a word to the wise, guys. The ROV operator has said there's a lot of Moray Eels around the wreckage, so be aware! Over."

If it was close enough for *Star Hercules* to execute the recovery, it could only mean one thing. It was the helicopter that had just flown Brian out to the dive vessel. The same one that had been returning Geoff to the beach. He couldn't be sure and didn't feel compelled to ask. Due to the haste of his hiring and arrival on the *Star Hercules*, Brian was whisked of the helideck just after greeting Geoff, below the whirling rotor blades. His new dive supervisor, Richard Clarke, a tall, anodyne man with jowls that drooped from his chin and twitched when he spoke, gave Brian a truncated tour through the inner workings of the vessel. The ship was only four years old but looked at least double that. The maintenance regime was non-existent if the rust on the O-rings, fitted over the seal between the bell and compression chambers, was an indication. The frayed lift wire attached to the bell and the corroded racking containing thousands of canisters of gas were just as an unnerving sight – as was meeting his new colleague, Ron. Charles hadn't told Brian about Ron's full title within the company – Red Mist Ron. He was a tattooed, pig-iron tough Scottish ex-military diver in his forties, which in itself wasn't uncommon. What was unusual was his impatient nature and intense, burning eyes. Richard wasn't as fastidious a supervisor as Kaare: the hip flask of whiskey in Ron's lap were evidence of this. The soap-on-a-rope and bottle of Brut aftershave on the seat next to him was his toiletry bag. With curly ginger hair and a flushed complexion, he explained that diving wasn't his first choice of career:

"Were you in the forces, Brian?" Ron abruptly asked his new colleague. All his words growled through clenched teeth. He radiated violent mental imbalance.

"God, no. I just missed national service. I guess you were?"

"Aye, in the Navy. I tried to rejoin for the Falklands War earlier this month but they said I was too old for active service. So I'm stuck here with you!"

"Why did you want to rejoin anyway?"

"I wanted to kill more people!" Ron growled with regret. His raging stare could de-bone a man.

"Why did you leave in the first place?" Brian dared.

"I was discharged for being too violent!"

The temperature was rising in the chamber, which was normal during press down as the pressure increased on the divers. When Richard signalled the end of the press down, Brian was pleased the announcement provided an interruption to an awkward conversation. For the sake of all humankind, particularly the Argentinean armed forces, Ron was best kept stored underwater, Brian thought.

"OK. We are now at working depth. Divers standby," Richard crackled.

"I would like Ron to be Bellman for this dive, he is used to it and this is your first time out here, Brian. Are you OK to continue, Diver One?" Richard was just about to ask the question again, when the confirmation came. He didn't tell Diver One that he was aware it was Geoff and the pilot due for recovery. But he didn't have to. Brian had pretty much reached the same conclusion and butterflies of foreboding were fluttering in his abdomen.

"I'll do it. Don't worry."

"And Ron is happy to be Bellman?"

"Aye," Ron shouted, in time with his irate jab at the transmit button.

After opening the door, the bell partially flooded owing to the disparity between the storage depth and actual depth of the recovery sight. Ron spun a valve open in the bell to increase the pressure until the water level dropped below the exit. Brian closed the clasp on the housing connecting the helmet and the rubber neck scarf while Ron connected his umbilical and checked the bailout tank on Diver One's back.

"Diver One testing comms."

"Can hear you loud and clear topside, Diver One."

Brian descended the steps out of the bell in as sangfroid a manner as possible, "Diver One entering water."

"Don't forget about the eels, Diver One. You should be able to see the light on the ROV that has a fix on the chopper?"

Even at three hundred metres, there was ample light to determine the ROV itself. And the long, banana yellow eels where tangled in an angry swarm, attracted to the wreckage. But they were nothing his trusty rig spanner and hand torch hadn't dealt with in the past. When working in such company, Brian preferred to drop to the bottom as soon as possible and start working as the resultant cloud of sediment stirred up would envelope him from view. And it also meant that if there was something out there in the abyss that would tempted to eat Brian, he wouldn't know before it happened, which was the way he preferred it.

"Diver One on the bottom now." Each sentence was interrupted by an inhalation or exhalation every bit as loud as his helium induced soprano vocal chords. "Making my way to the wreckage now. And yes, there are a fucking lot of eels."

"Roger that, Diver One. When you are ready and in position, please inform and we will drop the crane down to you when ready."

"OK, nearly there."

"We have attached lift bags to the crane for the bodies, Diver One. You'll just have to remove them, OK?"

His deepest fears were confirmed. The helicopter lay on its right side. The glossy black finish was scarred and twisted and all the windows smashed – only jagged fragments remained tight in the edges of their frames. The tail section was snapped off and lay rotor-less, some ten metres away. The tubular skids the helicopter ordinarily stood on were mangled in every angle imaginable. Entombed inside was a single body, lifeless and stiff.

"Bellman, I need a few more feet of umbilical. I can't reach the crane wire."

The diving supervisor seconded Brian's request, "feed Diver One more umbilical, Bellman."

"Aye."

Brian tried to open the two left doors but both had got jammed shut during the impact. The only way to recover the body was through the smashed windscreen, the pilot was lost and no longer occupying the cockpit. Diver One pulled himself into the cabin to recover his friend. In the testosterone-fueled offshore world, disagreements were settled with fists. And you did not emote – 'weak' guys stuck in the memory of dive supervisors and operators, for the wrong reason. But three hundred metres down, in the thick of a swarm of eels, what the dive supervisor couldn't see on the ROV monitor were the tears in Diver One's eyes. Tears that couldn't be wiped away. But the emotion in his voice was obvious.

"Only able to recover one body. It's fucking Geoff. Don't know where the pilot is. I have had a look but the current is pretty strong so he's probably gone."

"OK. Proceed with recovery and send him up and then we'll attach the lifting wire."

Brian tried to keep his damp, salty eyes closed when manhandling Geoff through the cockpit, which was filled with dislodged seat cushion and sections of interior fittings. He closed his eyes wherever possible, so Geoff's haunting expression wouldn't linger too long in the memory. Before beginning to inflate the lift bag that Geoff was attached, Brian tied himself to the wreckage with a lanyard. Otherwise, he had no way of bracing himself against a rapid ascent to the surface Geoff's remains were about to undergo.

"Just inflating the lift bag now. Body is attached," he announced, trying to maintain emotional composure while still grasping his friend. Geoff began to move upwards with the lift bag so Brian held on as long as he could to get a final few extra litres of inflation. Diver One opened his hand, releasing Geoff who was in full rigor mortis. Along with his bubbles, Brian watched Geoff rise up toward the lights. The silky eels moved around the body's trajectory as it spun beneath the air-lift. As Geoff neared the surface, Diver One raised an angled salute at the side of his helmet and mouthed the following;

"See you my friend."

"What was that Diver One?" Richard enquired.

"Nothing topside. Interference I think. Geoff should be at the surface now. I'll go connect the crane to the baastard."

"Thanks Diver One. OK. I can see you on the monitor. It's the other side of the wreckage."

"OK, on my way."

On the far side of the wreckage, at the limit of his umbilical and reaching for the crane hook, he wasn't concerned by the first tug, blaming it on an irregular movement of the ship transferring through his taught lifeline. The second jolt was harder and more serious, pulling him to the sea floor. The flow of hot water into his suit stopped first. The third tug came just as he was getting to his feet and dragged him backwards. He tried to brace himself by driving his gloved hands into the seafloor, the way the clouds of sediment stirred and flew away in the opposite direction told him he was being pulled against the current.

Brian's jaw was extended further than any other time in his life as he asked, "Topside, what the fuck is down here? I'm getting dragged around like a ragdoll? Is the ship moving?"

Before the answer came, his umbilical jerked backwards again and he lost communications with the vessel. The cold around him was starting to bite at the extremities, his hands and feet were soon numb. As it dragged against the jagged razors of glass of the wreckage, one more heave severed the power to his head torch. The only line of umbilical still functioning was the most important, the one feeding his gas. But even that had been partially ruptured.

"Negative, Diver One..................Diver One, please respond!"

From his dials, Richard the supervisor could see Diver One was losing gas from his umbilical but wasn't to know that was the only one intact. Effectively deaf and merely armed with a torch in one hand and crane hook in the other, Brian scrambled to connect the crane around the prop shaft of the helicopter. A request for Red Mist Ron to get into the water to rescue Brian had also passed without reply, leading Richard to believe the bell had also lost communications. Tracing the umbilical back to the bell, Brian passed his ruptured lifeline and his eyes widened as he held the impacted section in his left hand, he was amazed he was still alive. The piscatorial culprit nowhere to be seen.

"Fuck. Tell them to lift the crane. It's connected. What's wrong with you, Ron?"

Shaking from the cold, Brian emerged back into the bell and was presented with another emergency. The Bellman was more in need of rescue than Diver One was. Down on his haunches, Red Mist Ron was holding a bleeding mouth and groaning muffled curses. Ron had seemed capable of starting an argument in an empty bell, but a punch-up seemed unlikely, even for him. His bottom molar had decayed beneath the crown over a tooth and with the extra pressure needed to unflood the bell, the minute amounts of air inside the tooth had exploded. With it had gone the crown, more of the fetid tooth and some surrounding gum.

13. East Indiaman

Brian had fulfilled his diving part of the arrangement for *Highroller* with Terry. Diving with scuba tanks and a knife on the first dive, Terry had used the ride out to the wreck site to tell its new owner *Highroller*'s quirks and abilities, and to say his goodbyes. At low tide, Terry tied *Highroller* to the marker buoy and Brian traced the slippery rope down forty metres to retrieve the net. The visibility was poor, down to a grubby two metres and less once the sediment was stirred up. Terry's net had snagged tightly on three of six hull ribs that were exposed. The four-sided timbers were a foot square and angled proud of the seabed by a metre, the six timbers gave Brian an idea of the size of the wreck, obscured as it was by cubed polystyrene floats and ropes that once attached to Terry's fishing boat. Brian cut the green net free with as little use of his knife as possible, keeping the repair bill as low as possible. Apart from the ribs, he saw no other evidence of a wreck on the brief dive as he had to include a brief decompression stop. He just saw mounds and depressions, the row of ribs, some outlines and traces of rust imprinted on the seabed and that was it.

"There's a wreck down there, right?" Terry asked, while helping Brian get back on *Highroller*.

"Yeah, it looked like it." Brian confirmed as he removed his weight belt and unfastened the metal buckles holding the crutch flap which when released, resembled a beaver's tail.

"You forgot the cut the buoy line though?"

Brian hadn't forgotten. He wanted to revisit what was alleged to be the *Dalhousie* when he was more organised, so had re-attached it to the closest timber. "Oh shit. Sorry. Pass my coat will you, Terry?" As Terry brought the pile of clothes Brian had changed out of into his diamond patterned wetsuit, he continued. "You seem pretty knowledgeable about the wreck, Terry?"

"Yeah we think it's the *Dalhousie*. Went down in 1853 bound to Melbourne having never really lost sight of land from the Channel. What a bastard, eh?"

From the final resting place of the *Dalhousie*, sixteen miles WSW of Beachy Head, the coastline was a mere strip on the bobbing horizon.

"Yeah," Brian replied as he struggled to pull both wrists from his wetsuit. "What type of ship was it, Terry?"

"It's an East Indiaman."

"So what's that?"

"Those ships used to travel between the UK and the east. Singapore, Burma, India. That kind of thing. Bringing back all sorts." The information Terry was revealing was only kindling Brian's appetite. "A local salvage company knows about this wreck and have tried to find it."

With Brian's help, they heaved the net through the unzipped awning into *Highroller*'s cockpit. Their only catch of the day was some seaweed, a crab and a metal stake, two metres long and thirty millimeters in diameter. Fragments of wood were attached along its length, soft and brittle after a hundred and thirty years under The Channel. Judging by the turquoise colour of the bent stake, it was made of or coated in copper.

Along the coast, plans were well advanced to raise the *Mary Rose* up from eleven metres of water, one hundred kilometres west of the *Dalhousie*. The Tudor warship had sunk 437 years before in 1545, during an engagement with an invading French fleet. The raising of the flagship of King Henry VIII's navy, due to commence later that year, was generating a lot of public interest and media attention. Along with hundreds of other volunteer divers, Brian had worked on the *Mary Rose* after its initial discovery in 1971, two miles south of the entrance to Portsmouth Harbour.

Margaret Rule had been the chief archeologist on the project who was qualified to dive but was dismissive of divers who lacked an archeological background, no matter what their level of aptitude for removing and documenting artifacts was. Mrs. Rule had come in with government money and took over. She was an extremely driven woman who proved a bad match for a laid-back commercial diver like Brian. And he left the project soon after she became a member of the government's advisory committee on historic wrecks, despite her obvious talent. One man's determination is another man's pushy, domineering and headstrong nature.

The diving provided Brian with the adventure and the excitement: the historical research brought the interest. It fascinated Brian that all this potentially lucrative history, some of it myth and some researchable in public archives, was just strewn across the sea bed. By the time *Highroller* was back in the refuge of Newhaven marina, Terry's silence had been secured with a handshake on a 5% share of any profits from the wreck, by way of a finder's fee. Brian was increasingly aware that he needed projects to sustain himself after his offshore diving career ended. It was a natural progression on from dangerous diving to salvage leader. He wanted the *Dalhousie* for himself. He wanted his own *Mary Rose*.

Brian was 85% certain of the identity of the wreck, as the metal stake was confirmed in his research as a common method for securing decking or bulkhead planking on 19th century ships. The copper stakes would be heated until they were malleable before being driven through pre-drilled holes which were offset and then capped with a cold brass washer that was hammered into place. He was certain enough to commit himself financially to at least a few more visits to the wreck. Along with the imminent salvage projects in Morocco and Mauritania, he was speculating to accumulate after he was finished with diving.

It was May 1982 and six months of fair conditions lay ahead in the Channel in which he could explore, measure, excavate and confirm the wreck as the *Dalhousie*. Brian had had to serve a short-lived sabbatical back in his country of origin to apply for a residency permit in Brazil. It was long enough to rent an apartment in Brighton, adding to his rental portfolio of irate landlords in Cassis and Cabo Frio. There was also a court case to pursue after receiving yet another maintenance invoice for the Maserati. In their estimation, a whole new engine had to be fitted, to the tune of £4000. In Brian's estimation, they had fucked up the previous engine as they were more used to fixing Ford Escorts, so he wasn't liable for the cost of a new motor. The faults so numerous, the disputed estimate was a three-page report. If there was one thing Brian disliked more than bad mechanics, it was British public schoolboy lawyers.

After his initial dive to release Terry's nets and that first sight of the wooden ribs, time that would have been better spent researching the wreck had been consumed with fitting out and moving *Highroller* to Cassis. Then he devoted himself to growing a full beard and drinking as much cognac as was necessary for a worldly man pondering his future. The wreck had lain there for a hundred and thirty years already, and with Terry's lips financially sealed, it would still be there in the spring. Then the period of contemplation had been thoroughly shattered by the call from Geoff to work in Brazil. 26 Brunswick Square was a penthouse apartment in the north east corner surrounding Brunswick Park on three sides with regency townhouses that predated the sinking of the *Dalhousie*. His view from his balcony were filled with the columns, porticos and sash windowed facades facing the square and the sea through the far end of the central green.

Having already bought a Land Rover for land-based errands and chartered a barge named *Mount* out of Newhaven Harbour, Salvamar Diving and Salvage sprang into action with the delivery of a wet-bell (or open-bell). These were different to the enclosed, pressurised bells. They were fed air from the surface, and looked like nothing more than an open-sided or well ventilated telephone box with a clear plastic dome for a roof. The air pocket created by the dome afforded the working divers a refuge and the ability to communicate with the surface, should the communications to Brian's helmet fail. His favourite driven and headstrong woman, Anne, had proven extremely resourceful during Brian's absence in South America. *Highroller* had been shipped down to Gibraltar, ready for the crossing to Morocco. She had charmed the use of the bell from her employer, Comex. She even ran Salvamar's human resources department after the introduction of Lolly, her young cousin. Organised at very short notice, what Lolly lacked in diving experience, he compensated for with energy and a keen willingness to learn the art of salvage. His prominent nose and narrow lips were common Roman features. He bounced around the deck of the salvage barge in his tight jeans, colourful polo shirts and tasselled deck shoes, while a compact cassette personal stereo was hanging proudly from his waist belt, connected to fragile looking foamy headphones that sat on his shoulders.

With much scratching at his beard, Brian walked Lolly through his duties working topside on a salvage barge – not least of which was fetching lunchtime fish and chips from shore in the rib dinghy that served as the tender. Thereafter, the constant monitoring of the radio was paramount. Brian could do the first stages of work on the wreck, with some help floating above him. Tools would have to be sent down the buoy line and air-bags managed at the surface.

"So, Lolly. You just have to man the radio when I'm down there. I'll lower the bell the first time so you can see how to bring it up."

"OK, Bri-yon! You must show me!" Lolly pronounced Brian's name in the same way as his older cousin, which made him hard to dislike in Brian's eyes.

Brian's thick red diving suit appeared purple underwater due to its pea-green hue, but the visibility was good. From his diving harness hung an open-reel tape measure, two mesh bags and a wooden handled trowel for shifting heftier stones and aggregates. The seabed around the *Dalhousie* was a uniformly undulating beige clay with chalk outcrops and smooth limestone rocks. More of the wreck had been exposed after another winter's scouring by the currents and tides. It had been well preserved by an anoxic seam of mud and silt, the same medium that had preserved what remained of the Mary Rose so impressively. Fanning away the muddy deposits with his hand, Brian begun to recognise more of the copper pins and banks of ballast stones that dotted the site. A large stern section that could only have been unearthed the previous winter, was covered in what appeared to be a yellow sheet metal. If left long enough undisturbed, every wreck will decay to leave only stains on the seabed. But ribs were now protruding on both sides of the wreck, like a gigantic fish skeleton, gave a rough width of eight metres. A lone unused anchor, equidistant to the stern on the opposing side of the ribs, indicated the length of the wreck. Despite being capsized on the surface, the remaining weight of the cargo in the hold of the *Dalhousie* had evidently settled her flat on the sea floor.

14. Back to Brazil

With a new residency permit safely in his passport and the *Dalhousie* project advancing, Brian crossed the Atlantic once again, in order to fund his salvage projects. In his absence, Lolly would be fabricating the deck of the barge in preparation for a minimum two-man dive team later in the summer. Red Mist Ron was seemingly still receiving dental treatment, so Brian was paired with Malcolm Ferguson, who was from South Africa, but of Scottish stock. Despite an appearance every bit as tough as Ron, Malcolm was cut from softer, more amenable cloth. He was a little taller than Brian but he had a similar build and a magnificent fair moustache. His coiled hair was receding slightly above each temple, leaving a spit of hair on his crown. They both shared an easygoing humour and outlook on life, although Malcolm had married, unlike Brian.

Malcolm had also worked in the North Sea with a different operator, but South Africans were treated as second class owing to their willingness to work for lower hourly rates than those based more locally. Brian and Malcolm were both rugby fans and were more than a test for each other at backgammon. As the diving bell descended to two hundred and fifty metres below the Atlantic, prior to the first dive together, they cheerily exchanged who they knew in the industry all the way up to management level.

"Did you also work for Comex?"

"No, I worked for Global Diving Services out of Norway," Malcolm said. Brian was a little unaccustomed to the accent and combined with the effect of the helium, had to concentrate more than usual. "But we did get two managers turn up from Comex before I left. Two French guys."

Brian moved his head back in realization, "Were they called Arnaud and Gabriel? Or something like that?" he asked.

"Ja, that's right."

"Oh, fuck. You know what they did? At Comex, I mean?"

"No," Malcolm replied, widening his eyes in curiosity.

"God, if it's the same pair. They embezzled a load of money for years. Two auditors were sent out from France to the office in Aberdeen. When they arrived one morning, right, they were stuck in a side office with all the accounts to keep them busy while that bloody Gabriel and Arnaud cleared out their desks. They went and told the auditors they had an important lunch meeting with a client which would take a few hours and asked if they had enough account information to keep them busy while Arnaud and Gabriel were away. Then they promptly fucked off to Amsterdam, via the company's bank branch to empty the account."

"How do you know?"

"Because I was in the same brothel in Amsterdam with a couple of guys, six months later. After we told the girls there that we were divers, they said they had had two French divers in six months before requesting a bloody champagne bath with them!" Malcolm was seized in a spasm of incredulous laughter as Brian finished the story: "One of the girls said one of them asked to have champagne poured over his dick as they filled the bath. And they only had the little bottles, too"

The mirth was rudely interrupted by Richard, the dive supervisor.

"OK, two minutes to working depth, chaps. Over."

"Roger," Malcolm confirmed.

"We have a long day ahead. We'll split the bell duties, so who's in the water first? Over."

"I'll take the first four hours," Brian replied.

"OK, so Malcolm will do the second stint? Over."

"Ja."

"Very good. Carry on. Please confirm when Diver One is on the bottom? I'm opening Diver One's gas supply on my panel guys, over."

"OK. Diver One gas supply open in bell. Diver leaving bell."

An ROV had remained at the worksite during the shift change: now it relayed flickering monochrome images of Diver One feeding out his umbilical before exiting the diving bell. After both his feet caused a cloud of sediment to explode, Brian was more concerned with an enormous crustacean that reared up as he reached the seabed. It had numerous huge claws snapping, pulsating gills, wailing feelers and its spiny body arched aggressively backwards. A wide-eyed Brian reacted swiftly in manner default to many commercial divers – he whacked it with a rig spanner, much to the dismay of marine biologists and researchers. Species such as the snapping, horny monster he had disturbed were probably unknown to science and would remain unrecorded.

"Diver One on the bottom," Brian said belatedly. He spun around in the direction of the worksite and got a much larger fright. A lazy floating grouper fish, khaki-coloured and balancing on a pair of dancing pectoral fins was as tall as Brian and blocking his path. Its two inquisitive eyes were either side of a mouth large enough to inhale Diver One. Fresh from his warm-up sparring with the massive shellfish, a combination of a left cross with the spanner followed by a right uppercut with a hand torch moved the huge fish on its way, back into the gloom where Brian knew all manner of creatures were normally lurking. In the fish world a diving bell appeared to be an industrial-sized chandelier that occasionally dropped into their dark habitat and required investigation after they were attracted to the lights on the underside.

Before transferring into the bell, Malcolm and Brian had both read the daily briefing and viewed the schematic diagram passed through the airlock hatch. The assignment for the long day was to attach new guide posts onto a wellhead, in preparation for the fitting of new plant on the structure. The posts would be dropped down to Diver One in turn by crane, after each of the four fixing bolts were secured. The first had been fitted and Brian was moving to the next location to await the arrival of the second guide post. His air supply had been difficult to demand since leaving the bell. Then an oily, metallic taste permeated his helmet.

"Topside, this is Diver One. Nearly in position for the second guide post. I've got a funny taste on my airline. Like diesel. Please check up there?" he asked, just before he started to experience the symptoms of nitrogen narcosis.

Richard reviewed the dials and readings across the whole of the distribution panel he was sat in front of while guiding the divers, "All looks good topside, Diver One." Richard checked with Malcolm, on the same radio channel. "Bellman, is everything OK with you?"

"No problems here. All systems good, topside," Malcolm confirmed. But he was incorrect.

Owing to an undetected leakage on Richard's instrument panel, along with a normal supply of heliox gas through Brian's airline, a 97%/3% oxygen to helium mixture, he was also being fed air from the surface, a less palatable 21%/79% oxygen to nitrogen. While diving on air tanks, even recreational scuba divers knew that narcosis could be experienced at only forty metres, and Brian was working two hundred metres deeper. The high amount of nitrogen swiftly brought on the disorientating effects of narcosis. His vision began to shrink slowly down to a pinpoint, which in such twilight conditions, translated to almost total blindness. He was increasingly at the mercy of the situation, as his body was in the early stages of blacking out. A light-headed confusion filled his mind, each breath shallower than the previous as Brian suspected he was poisoning himself with each inhalation.

"Diver One, please respond? I can't see you on my screen?" Richard asked, routinely.

Brian was no longer able to properly concentrate. His hearing was affected next, as his senses gradually continued to shut down. Each sound echoed around his head as he struggled to process the situation. His heart begun to flutter as if it was unable to supply his body with the blood it required. Each irregular beat felt akin to an orchestral bass drum booming arhythmically in his chest. Perspiration poured from his skin and could be felt in the corners of his blind eyes. The smell of oil continued in his helmet, his mouth and down into his chest. Stupefied and barely able to reason, let alone move, all Brian could think to do was rely on his muscle fibres to get him back to the bell, if he took another full breath, he would most likely black out completely. He was connected to the bell via his umbilical so his diminished senses were irrelevant. He just needed the strength to pull himself up his umbilical and into the bell. He didn't wait for the taste in his helmet to clear or switch supply to the small bailout tank on his back, he just needed to return to the relative safety of the bell. On the verge of losing consciousness, he pulled, grabbed and tugged himself towards the lights, his weakness and confusion almost overwhelming him. The term 'lifeline', normally used as a second name for the umbilical, was never so fitting as at that moment.

"Bellman, I don't have a visual on Diver One and he is not responding and I'm not hearing him breathing?"

"Roger, topside. Diver One not in bell. Do I start a recovery?"

"I think you should prepare Bellman, yes. Unless Diver One responds in the meantime."

"OK, topside. Opening Diver Two gas supply." Malcolm confirmed, unaware it was the source of Diver One's silence.

Brian could hear voices on the radio, but was unable to comprehend who they were or what they were saying. But they seemed to be getting louder and Brian couldn't even form words, let alone a sentence. Each pull with his arms harder than the last, each thump in his chest felt terminal. Hand over hand, heave after heave, all he could focus on was climbing that lifeline. That was the only way he would stay alive.

By the way the umbilical was bouncing up out of the exit, Malcolm could that see Brian was climbing back to the bell. Brian brushed past the clump weight suspended below the bell and knew he had only a couple of metres left when he lugged himself on the circular stage directly under the bell door. Delirious and feeble, he pushed his torso upward to swing his feet beneath him.

Malcolm was about to exit the bell and straddled the door while he hurriedly uncoiled his umbilical off its storage hook. Looking down through the aperture, he could see Brian labouring up the final few steps into the bell. Malcolm dropped to his knees and reached down for a firm hold on straps of the harness over Brian's shoulders and pulled. Aware Brian was struggling to move freely, Malcolm got him high enough into the bell that his arms could extend. Immediately, Brian pointed to his helmet, urgently jabbing his crooked index finger towards his eyes. The Bellman swiftly released the locking mechanism on the helmet as Diver One craned his neck backwards to aid its removal.

"Topside. Diver One is now back in the bell."

"OK, Bellman. Is there a problem?"

"Maybe?"

Those first few gasps of air tasted sweet and clean, drawn deep by an impatient diaphragm, and thus began the slow reclaim of his senses. If he hadn't taken the evasive action, he would have been joining young Mickey and Geoff up in the heavens. Were Brian a rookie diver, he would most likely also be hanging limp on his umbilical. For all his joking around and apparently off-the-cuff demeanour, Brian had always kept his ears open so he could learn from others, even from their mistakes, and this had saved him.

The temporary blindness gradually subsided which made it difficult to open his eyes in the comparative dazzling lights in the bell. The pressure on his chest lifted and his brain began to recognise sounds and speech patterns. All the symptoms abated after a couple of minutes with his helmet removed, slightly stunned he had come so close.

It was as close as he had ever come to dying with his helmet on.

15. Way out

After the last incident and at 42 years old, entering his twelfth year in commercial diving, Brian experienced second thoughts on his career. He pondered why he had returned to the industry he had only recently exited and his motivation. He already had reservations about taking the contract in Brazil, coming as it did at a point when he had mentally bid farewell to commercial diving. He could feel a difference in his body and how it recovered from the rigours of the profession. The years had taken their toll on Brian. In the warm, clammy confines of the compression chamber, ear infections, the bane of divers, were commonplace. Skin rashes wouldn't clear up and the greater working depths placed extra demands on the body. Stored at a pressure of 350psi, the equivalent ambient worksite pressure of 240m, performing any task underwater was like working in heavy custard. Every movement, such as tightening bolts on subsea structure or fighting off a grouper, took extra effort than it would on the deck of the *Star Hercules*. At 240m, there was close to twenty-four atmospheres of pressure, twenty-four times that exerted on the surface.

Brian had been disguising these concerns with his usual charm and humour, but he wasn't the same inside anymore. His apprehension was forever rising, each exit from the bell being a little harder than the last. Feeling somewhat trapped knowing he would be diving again the next day, Brian had no choice but get back on the horse. Even though it was a horse he feared had a loose saddle and would fall at the first hurdle. If he requested a way out, the door to the industry would most likely slam firmly behind him and he would never find a way back in again, even as a supervisor. And regardless of the state of his investments and projects, if he was dead, there would be no payback anyway, no return on the time and money he had invested. Not to mention the potential loss of his playboy assets: the value of his Maserati and *Highroller* were both leveraged into the deals.

The divers had little influence on the running of the ship from inside the bell, but at least he had faith in Malcolm. The respect was mutual. Malcolm was taken by the way Brian maintained the wherewithal to drag himself back to the bell during their last dive.

Phone calls were replacing letter writing, and telephone receivers were increasingly common inside decompression chambers, a relative luxury allowing more immediate contact to the outside world with family, friends and loved ones. The helium's effect on the vocal chords meant whoever was on the other end of the line had to be fluent in 'canary'. Anne was the closest to a loved one Brian had. And the nearest to a business partner and personal assistant to boot.

"Bri-yon, the boat was shipped to Gibraltar, ready to move to Morocco, but Spanish customs have impounded it in Algeciras!"

"Oh, that's a baastard." Brian replied with his eyes closed. It wasn't the news he needed to hear. Just when the urge to leave the industry was at its most acute, the doors to opportunities away from offshore diving were beginning to slam shut at just the wrong time. "I had to get across to Morocco before the end of the year. And all my spare cash is tied up on that one job."

"I'm sorry I cannot help more, but you have to get the boat yourself."

"I'll think of something. I might ask if Bill to come down and help: you remember Bill from when we moved the boat down?"

"But of course. Funny guy."

"OK, divers prepare to transfer to the bell please," Richard asked his divers to prepare.

Brian nodded silently towards Malcolm, indicating he also heard the instruction "Anne, I have to go. I'll call you tomorrow, OK."

The bell was fixed to the top of the pressurised living chambers, a circular upward trunking which finished flush with the rear deck and Brian and Malcolm climbed up to take their positions, after the previous shift had withdrawn to their own separate chamber. The daylight pouring through the tiny porthole was the sole natural light they saw during their weeks of confinement. Once in the water and descending to the worksite, the porthole shifted through ever darkening shades of sapphire. But they didn't reach the water on that occasion as the dive was aborted before the bell even got wet. A few irregular crunches transmitted through the lift cable as the crane begun to lift the bell clear of the living chamber. The O-Rings securing the seal were removed by diving technicians on the deck of the *Star Hercules*. As the bell swung a metre above the circular seal, the lift wire snapped, dropping the pressurised bell back onto to the main chamber. Mass panic broke out among the technicians as they inspected for damage and crucially, leaks.

Inside the bell, a very shaken pair of caged canaries, Brian and Malcolm, gave each other an inquisitive stare as they assessed their situation. The bell appeared to have survived the impact. There was no loud hissing around the bell door which would indicate a damaged seal and loss of pressure. Even a partial leak could induce a life-threatening bend as the pressure would reduce in excess of that recommended in dive compression tables.

However, they weren't to know if the seal on the top of the chamber had been damaged, and were unaware if the divers in the other interconnecting chambers had been affected by a rapid decompression. Although if this had happened they wouldn't have known much about their passing, they would simply have exploded. In a split second each molecule of gas in their bodies would expand relative to the amount of atmospheres they were stored at. Whether sleeping or entering and exiting the bell, their lungs would be the first thing to explode. If you were unfortunate enough to be in the vicinity of the leak, after exploding it was likely your mortal remains would be squeezed through the gap and scattered beyond the chamber, such were the forces at work. The only saving grace in this situation was that the passing would be immediate, at least. Especially if you were asleep.

Within the bell, the impact was so forceful, it was hard to envisage the chamber hadn't sustained some damage. But the fevered yelling from the technicians circling the bell soon begun to subside. Brian and Malcolm took this as the emergency was over and all had survived somehow, if only though good fortune.

"OK, dive aborted," Richard advised his divers in the bell, confirming the obvious.

"What the fuck happened there?" Brian asked.

"Lift wire broke, chaps. No harm done. We are just getting the spare attached now."

"Fuck's sake, Richard."

"Sorry guys."

"Is the seal damaged?"

"We don't think so. Better it happens up here on deck than down there, hey guys." It was a somewhat misplaced and flippant remark to two divers who would rather it hadn't happened at all.

"Easy for you to say. You should try it in here!"

"We don't want to try to lift you guys using the bell's umbilical, so just hang tight there. Won't be long," Richard's speech was staggered as he received whispered reports from staff members in the control room. Both divers shook their heads in inaudible unison, Brian with his jaw pronounced with annoyance. The most conscientious diver or divers could be undone by a poor crew, or as Brian had observed of other unprofessional crews from his past, "If they haven't killed you yet, they fucking will do!"

The ungalvanised spare cable was only a spare, as the same failure had happened two months earlier. A repair of sorts had been carried out before it was coiled on the open rear deck of the *Star Hercules*. Sixty days of water spray had worked on the individual strands, the salt accelerating the corrosive process, affecting the strength and flexibility. It passed a hasty visual inspection before re-entering service to successfully position the bell to allow a transfer next day. The spare cable gave no indication of impending failure when first taking the load of the bell. From inside the bell the following morning, it felt sound as Brian and Malcolm were once again lifted clear of the chamber and deposited through the surf.

"OK, guys. We can do the job now we expected to do yesterday. All OK in the bell there, Bellman?"

As Bellman once again, Malcolm replied for them both, "Yes topside, just let us know when we are on the bottom. The new cable is making a strange sound. Keeps pinging?"

"All looks good with the cable. The one which broke yesterday has been repaired so we have our redundancy back, you'll be pleased to know."

A few minutes passed before Diver One was given permission to leave the bell to begin working. Richard gave the all clear, "Divers on the bottom. You should be around five metres above the floor there."

As a precaution and to satisfy his curiosity, Brian headed for the top of the bell on his return, to take a look at the new cable. He was met by the shocking sight of all but two strands flared widely either side of the repair. His experience reminded Brian to be mindful of his diving helmet around the twisted strands, divers had been killed in these very circumstances by errand wire strands becoming caught in the locking mechanism between the helmet and the neck scarf. Worse still was when the mechanism was inadvertently opened by head movement when a strand got snagged between the lock's body and release handle. Once released under water, you were dead. No vision, communication or air to breathe, just a swift, sightless demise.

"Topside, this is Diver One. You are not lifting us back up on this cable. There's only two strands left. That noise we heard on the way down must have been the others breaking. I thought you said it had been replaced?"

"It was. Yesterday afternoon."

"And did you check it yourself afterwards?"

"No, Diver One, I didn't."

"Great. And now you can't lift the baastard back up?"

"I'll bring the ROV up to join you to get a visual. What do you suggest, from what you can see down there?"

"You're the supervisor and you're asking me what to do? I'm two hundred odd metres under bloody water and you want me to do your job too. What is this?" Richard remained silent, so Brian gave his summary. "Lower us down to the seabed, I'll detach the cable so you can pull it up and send down the one from yesterday. The one you say is repaired, right?"

"That will take some time, Diver One."

"Well, fucking get on with it then," Brian snapped impatiently.

Brian returned to Malcolm in the bell and sat out the two hours it took to swap the cable again. Just two souls in a metal sphere stranded on the ocean floor, totally dependent on a boat floating 240m above them and the thin tubes that linked between. In that time, Brian cemented his concerns. He had already removed his dead friend from the wreckage of a helicopter and could have died himself in both his previous dives. Now he was stuck on the seabed, waiting for a crane to become operational.

The redundant cable was fed down on the bell umbilical and Brian fed out only a few spools of lifeline, enough to reach to the fixing point on the top of the bell. With a short coil of rope in one hand and chuntering dissatisfaction to himself as he climbed, he attached the cable to the lifting-ring and, as a precaution, wound the rope around the lifting point and above the termination lug on the end of the cable that formed the loop several times before tying it off.

Malcolm passed on the good news when Diver One had returned, "Diver One back in bell, topside. You can commence lift now, but nice and slow please."

The diving bell had slightly clogged in the seabed during the delay and as the pressure grew on the lifting cable, the bell unplugged and shot up two metres like airline turbulence. After that, it was the most fraught ascent in a diving bell Brian had ever experienced. He knew that the real test was awaiting them above the surface, between the waves and the deck where gravity suddenly replaced buoyancy and the true weight would be loaded onto the lifting cable.

16. Research

An autumnal return to south coast of England had never been more appreciated after Brian's brushes with mortality in Brazil. The trees he could see from his penthouse were beginning the seasonal shift from abundant, verdant green to flat, dead brown. He turned his central heating on immediately, his apartment felt and smelled damp with the cold. He wouldn't be rushing back across the Atlantic for two months after requesting some leave, which provided eight weeks to delve deeper into the *Dalhousie* wreck. The shipwreck charts, archived accounts of the sinking, passenger lists and details of the ownership at the time he had requested were all encased in various sized envelopes, piled up behind his front door. They were given preference over anything that looked like it could be a bill. He had all the research essentials – coffee, tea, milk, sugar, cigarettes, cognac and an Italian bistro around the corner where he faithfully observed the 'Omar Sharif' diet of only one meal a day in a good restaurant.

The first account Brian read was of the sinking itself, relayed by the sole survivor, able seaman Joseph Reed: it seized Brian's interest instantly. The fact that the ship had sunk with the voyage in its infancy was troubling enough. But the fact that so many had perished who should have been saved in a busy shipping lane made every word of his account haunting. Mr Reed had survived for nearly eleven hours on an unstable chock, before being picked up and taken ashore by the twin-masted brig *Mitchel Grove*, the captain and crew of which showed him great kindness after his rescue. Throughout the harrowing time he had been stuck on the timber flotsam, he had heard the survivors succumb to terrified hypothermia or drown in the darkness, one by one. Just a single sinking represented as a mark on a shipwreck map, one of hundreds in what appeared to be a graveyard for ships. One sunken tomb lay seventy-five metres west of the *Dalhousie*, another only fifty metres to the north west. The *Dalhousie* was an Indiaman class of ship, a commercial frigate ferrying passengers to Australia, and one had never been salvaged before. The imminent raising of the *Mary Rose* had heightened the British public's interest in its maritime history, and Brian was hoping it would ease his job of raising funds for the salvage. But first he had to positively identify the wreck, and until he could, the initial salvage costs had to be covered from his own pockets.

Reading the account brought the wreck site alive for Brian. It included details of the cargo, valued at £100,00 in October 1853, which Brian estimated between £3,000,000 and £4,000,000 in October 1982. But there were no details in the ship's inventory, discovered amongst documents recovered from the abandoned quarter boat, just the overall insurance value. And only the insurance values of the ships' goods and those of individual passengers were quoted. Presumably it had been due for completion and registration in Plymouth, as seeing out the rough seas in The Channel took precedence.

Lolly had been busy fabricating the deck of the salvage barge *Mount* and only needed a couple more days to finish before they could leave port and start the investigation in earnest. It was enough time for Brian, the mysterious black sheep of the Worley family, to spend some rare time in Essex with his family. His mother, brother, sisters, nephews and nieces were all treated to drives in his exotic car, cups of tea, some bad cooking, pictures drawn at the request of his young family members, tales of his life in Brazil or Cassis and his latest projects. He'd be force-fed throughout by his mother, like a goose producing foie gras. But a subject never broached was his work: he didn't want his family to worry and certainly had no intention of laying a trail of anecdotal breadcrumbs which might lead his nephews to follow their enigmatic uncle. After his last ill-fated trip to Brazil, his mind had been made up that he also wanted out of commercial diving before it killed him. The *Dalhousie* could be the start of his way out of diving and on his own terms too.

He estimated it was a prudent time to go semi-public about the *Dalhousie* and contacted Margaret Rule. He had exited the *Mary Rose* project in its early stages but had at least done it on the best terms possible, so he still felt confident that Margaret would take his call and maybe even come and inspect whatever they recovered to identify the wreck. She was at the peak of her fame at that time, with the ear of her royal patrons and other luminaries of her archeological trust. Brian wasn't courting her patronage, just the camera lenses that would follow her. On the third attempt, he got through to her on the phone and explained his potential find, highlighting the urgency of salvaging what remained of the wreck before it broke up as it was already snagging fishing nets, so exposed were portions of the site. And no Indiaman ship had been salvaged before. He was canny enough to retain an ace up his sleeve to prevent her from wanting to assume any control of the *Dalhousie* project, as she had seized the mantle on the raising of the Mary Rose. Brian worked enough informal charm into his explanation for Margaret to agree to visit in November once the Mary Rose was back on dry land.

"Magic!" he said to himself with a mischievous smirk as he put the phone down. So he had some diving to do by day and by night, now he was tasked with research and finding a museum willing to exhibit the artefacts.

The *Mount* barge left Newhaven Harbour in earnest with a few final jobs to be completed en-route. Twenty metres in length and five broad, its open hold was covered over with planking, each painted a flat red with a white stripe at each end. The wet bell was connected to the small crane. The bilge pump was on continuously, drawing seawater out of the leaky hull. The shed-like bridge was set back above the rounded stern, next to a life-raft and a small one-person gas chamber for emergencies. On narrow worktops newly fitted to three sides inside the bridge sat communications equipment, sonar readers and a brace of large compasses. However, the undersized wooden wheel looked like Lolly had it stolen from the wall of a local yacht club or nautically themed restaurant.

It had previously just felt like a case of proving the identity of the pile of timbers and copper stakes. Having absorbed the whole story of the tragic sinking, diving down to explore a piece of subsea history, previously hidden beneath the waves, it was now very real. In his diving outfit, Brian was floating just above the same hull the family mentioned in Joseph Reed's statement had been washed into the sea.

Time was against them as it was autumn in The Channel, the swell was increasing to wintry norms and the currents were building beneath. They had to recover what they could in the short window before autumn turned into winter. The first few dives were spent mapping out the site before anything was recovered. A little more of the wreck was exposed and Brian saw what he thought was deck planking. The motherlode would be the recovery of a ship's bell or nameplate, something that would positively distinguish the *Dalhousie* from all the other wrecks down there. Other than that, it was a painstaking case of matching up what they recorded on the seabed with admiralty charts and ship design, both generally of the time and what was specifically known about the *Dalhousie* build. Persistent fanning and wafting through the central area of the site exposed the bezel of the ship's compass and brass mast-band through the clouds of sediment. As each encrusted item was recovered and taken up on deck with the same reverence as a cache of gold, Brian was building his case and his route out of diving.

Through Giuseppe, the owner of the Italian bistro near Brunswick Square, he had been introduced to a local salvage guru and fellow diner, Ray Todd. Ray told Brian he knew of an old wreck called the *Dalhousie* and had even dived many times in the area in search of it, but had been unable to locate it. From the description Ray gave over a Bolognese and glass of claret, Brian knew he had found the right boat. The dimensions matched, the metal pins were common boat building techniques of the period and the mast-band was representative of the diameter found on a ship of that scale. The more he learned and discovered, the more life it breathed into the wreck.

Day after day, the *Mount* barge chugged in and out of Newhaven, its course charted by a trail of acrid exhaust fumes. As the date with Margaret Rule was moving nearer, heightening the need for positive identification, Brian enlisted the help of a local scuba diving club. He could get a lot more bodies working on the wreck and apart from keeping them topped up with tea and fish & chips, they came along for free. These weekend warriors got to hang out with a bona fide saturation diver while living out their fantasies of diving on a wreck while Brian acquired some cheap labour. The increase in voluntary hands available made it possible to construct the beginnings of a transverse lifting frame over the wreck. A matching series of supports would then be established through shafts under the wreck, cut with high pressure water hoses. Once the upper and lower portions of the frame were connected as one, air-lift bags would be attached to the frame and inflated, raising the *Dalhousie* back into the light. A lifting pontoon would then be needed for the final heave out of The Channel and back to shore. But that would take more money than Brian could sustain. His pockets could only cover the initial stages of the salvage, so the focus was on demonstrating it was the *Dalhousie* and hope that enough money to raise what could prove a Victorian time capsule would follow. The last items to be recovered before the announcement were the pintles and gudgeons, a hinged assembly between the hull and the rudder, and the considerable stern section covered in the yellow metal sheeting. The weight of the latter caused the *Mount* barge to list markedly on its return to port.

During his evenings in Brunswick Place, he worked through all the information. His ashtray and cognac glass were perpetually brimming as he read the varying accounts of the sinking: cuttings from British and Australian newspapers; how the loss was recorded with the insurers Lloyds of London; the crew and individual crew members and most crucial of all; the rights to ownership of surviving relatives of John Allen, the ship's owner at the time of the disastrous sinking. Chartered by

White Horse Lines for paid passage to Sydney, only the passengers and able-seamen were documented. Her all-Indian crew were a legacy of the ship's original construction in the sub-continent prior to its entry into service. Although smuggling was rife on the open seas, Captain Butterworth's standing was beyond reproach. During his reputable years of service, he had never been party to any documented illicit behaviour.

On the night before Margaret Rule was due to visit Newhaven Harbour to authenticate what had been recovered, Anne arrived from Marseille on Brian's invitation. He was a little nervous on the eve of his big day and wanted some company around for moral support. At the same time, she could get to see her energetic cousin, who most days could be found bouncing along the deck boards covering the wide hull of the *Mount*. Once again in residence in Guiseppe's cosy bistro, the air thick with the smell of bitter, burnt garlic and charred meats, they poured glass after glass of burgundy.

"Bri-yon, but the beard, it suits you *non*?" Anne said of Brian's full beard, increasing flecked with grey strands among the still predominant black.

"Thanks. It's getting a bit itchy though."

"I like it."

"So the boat is now in Gibraltar. I just moved it last week with Bill before coming home. I forgot to tell you."

"Ah, *oui*. Such a nice guy. How is Bill?"

"Yeah, he's good."

"And the fine?"

"That's taken care of, too."

"OK, great. I can't wait to see what you have to show me tomorrow, Bri-yon. And to see Lolly too. Fantastic!"

"He's done well, Lolly. Was a bit of a baastard teaching him in the beginning."

"*Oui*, he is stubborn, like you!" Anne was joking but it was true. "But this wreck, it is so interesting *non*?"

"There's a lot of it. It can be boring sometimes on my own in the flat."

"I bet. But interesting?"

"Yeah, but the problem with history is you never bloody learn anything bloody new!"

17. Announcement

Stood just across from his penthouse white glossed front door, Brian and Anne were on their way to Newhaven Harbour, which was to the east along the coast. The polished checkerboard floor tiles continued down onto the steps of a spiral staircase with ornate Victorian ironwork, adjacent to the lift shaft. The passageway was dimly lit in the early winter morning gloom. Counting the lift up to the top floor by the mechanical thumps and grinds it made on its way, Anne turned to Brian and said something she had wanted to say for years. Out of the blue, she swivelled and dropped her chin so she could look into Brian's eyes above her glasses and said;

"Bri-yon, you know if you asked me to marry you, I would say yes, don't you?"

After his experience in Athens thirteen years before with Dora, he had vowed to never marry again. His lawyers had given up the trail of serving the divorce papers, so if Brian were to accept Anne's offer of matrimonial bliss, he would technically have had to become a polygamist to do so. While he slid the lift door open for his guest, he rebuffed Anne's offer as softly as he could, with his lower mandible extended, "Anne, you know I can't do that. Relationships are tricky for me. I definitely want it, but I need my space too, that's very important to me. Love inevitably causes pain and I had enough of that last time. You could find somebody more stable than me if you wanted, surely?" Brian was right, she probably could, but she didn't want to. She just wanted him to know how she truly felt, ever since he first arrived in Marseille at Budda.

And so approving was her father, Maximilian, that it was possible he would even stretch to pay Brian a dowry to marry his daughter.

Brian parked his Maserati out of sight for fear of appearing to be a 'Flash Harry', an accusation his father had perpetually leveled at him. He wasn't one for patting himself on the back too often, but he couldn't help but note how much things had changed for the better since his confinement at H.M.P. Lewes prison, just ten kilometres inland from Newhaven. He was dressed in a white shirt, dark V-necked jumper and leather jacket, his horseshoe moustache freshly re-cut that morning, unlike his greying windswept hair which fell over his ears and sat below his collar. Anne caught the eye of Lolly, who was already waiting for Brian to arrive and the two relatives immediately switched to a brisk form of French. Brian didn't understand a word, so he casually sloped off and prepared to exchange the company of one short, dark-haired, spirited woman for another. The *Mount* was moored tightly in its rented berth, the deck tidied and swept to shipshape level by Lolly. All the relics recovered from the wreck were displayed along the portside hull planking. The mast-band, compass bezel, pintles, gudgeons and copper stakes were there for all to see. The larger portion of stern had been offloaded from the *Mount* and moved to a disused corner of the harbour, but still in sight of the *Mount*.

Dr. Margaret Rule was no fool and wouldn't even have been in attendance if had she thought Brian was mistaken or bullshitting, or both. Regardless of her arrival, flanked by serious faced bald-headed reporters in suits, her manner seemed milder than what Brian remembered. "Good morning, Brian. It has been a long time. It looks like we have both been busy," she said.

"Hi Margaret, nice to see you. Thanks for coming along," Brian said while they shook hands next to the *Mount*. His esteemed visitor was wearing a lilac short-sleeved tunic and a 35mm camera hung on a strap around her neck. Her chestnut hair was shorter than Brian's and parted to the left, her fringe lifted up and down on the sea breeze. The lenses of her glasses were shaded out in the November morning light. "Well done with the *Mary Rose*, by the way. It was magic seeing it out of the water."

"Thanks, Brian," Margaret replied before clapping her hands together, "So what do you have to show me, Brian?"

Brian took her through the recovered artefacts and Margaret nodded encouragingly appraising each of them. Her knowledge was second to none and she knew well what she was looking at, but the *Mary Rose* was keeping her busy enough to not want to assume control of new endeavours. Brain was in the driving seat of this project, but was being deliberately coy about his confidence in the identity of the wreck: a game of marine archaeological poker, if you will. Brian ensured he was always visible when the cameras were pointing at Margaret, so as not to give the impression that the *Dalhousie* was anything other than his baby.

"You've done a good job of cleaning these up. I really think you are onto something, Brian."

"Well, we cannot be sure it is the *Dalhousie* as we have no conclusive proof yet. But it is an interesting find," Brian stated cannily, loud enough for the reporters to also hear. Her stock was high in the media: she brought the cameras but that didn't mean he was obliged to confirm anything. Speculation may summon Margaret and the reporters back a second time.

"There should be interesting objects down there. It reflects 19th century life in a way you cannot find anywhere else, it is a time capsule."

"We still haven't binned the theory that it could be spillage from a ship called the *Aristos* which went down a hundred and fifty metres away," Brian knew it wasn't, but that was for others to work out.

"Yes, in '67 wasn't it? I know the one. The wreck sits bolt up right now. Very well preserved."

"And it's not unknown for one wreck to found under another. It has happened before."

"Yes, true. There are so many out there. So much history."

"So we cannot be sure just yet."

"You know one of these has never been recovered before, don't you?" Margaret asked, hinting at the importance of Brian's find.

"Yeah I was aware of that. We have started to build a rudimentary lifting cradle using scaffold poles. But we can't do any more now until next year."

"Yes, you'll need one of those."

"Yeah, what is left of her won't have much structural strength."

"If it is the *Dalhousie* as you or we think, are there any owners? Or surviving relatives? Someone with a claim to the wreck I mean?"

His answer revealed his true confidence in his find, "I've gone through all the census records since 1843 and I don't think there are any surviving relatives. But I'm waiting for a few more details from the Public Record Office on that one."

"You may be onto something here, Brian," she repeated, wiping her hands dry on her denim skirt after inspecting the compass bezel more closely.

"I hope so."

"If you can prove it's the *Dalhousie*, your next step will be to raise the capital. If I were you, I would emphasise the historical significance and that the wreck be raised as a matter of urgency as another snagged fishing net could cause irreparable damage," Margaret said.

"Thanks, Margaret. I will bear that in mind. Magic."

"But what really fascinates me about shipping to Australia during this time is the mortality rate of the poor passengers. You know, you were less likely to survive on these ships than original ones carrying out the convicts. Imagine that? Horrendous! It's something like one in five children died during the voyage, that's twenty percent! Or the average, I mean. The adults were something like one in sixty, if memory serves. Frightening really."

She left soon afterwards with the reporters in tow. She was a good person to have involved, even if he intended to keep her on the periphery. She had afforded him exactly what he needed – her confirmation of the unconfirmed. A totemic spokeswoman for her field, well-seasoned in the art of persuading sponsors to inject funding, what with her royal connections through the *Mary Rose* project. He had handed Margaret his admission ticket into the world of historical wreck salvage and she had duly stamped it.

Anne was flying back to France the following morning and Brian was leaving for Brazil the day after that. He had seen the last of the *Dalhousie* for the year. There were more hours of darkness than daylight and The Channel was rarely clement. The wreck had been fully surveyed and the beginnings of the salvage operation had begun. A winters worth of tides may expose more of the wreck just as easily as cover it over again in a layer of silt. But anything of any value, precious metals and safes belonging to the ship or first class passengers were too heavy to be subject to the vicious currents. As the three dimensional structure of the hull would collapse into its footprint, heavy objects would only continue to sink that bit deeper into the sediment. The issue of weight versus gravity also applied to the stern section, which was resting at an awkward angle against a retaining brick wall. Without the means to move it, Brian decided it would be too heavy for anyone to consider shifting it.

18. Decompression

"This thing is fucking mental! It keeps coming at me."

An unfathomable, slender species of fish, over a metre in length, was perpetually ambushing Brian as he worked on a well-head. It's vast horizontal mouth was crammed with serrated teeth that Brian could hear snap shut with every feverish bite. It bumped and circled and rushed Diver One, even entangling itself in the loops of spare umbilical behind Brian that swayed in the currents. It was the last dive of a hitherto thankfully incident-free hitch back in Brazil, but now the piscatorial demon was relentlessly harassing Diver One. Both Malcolm the Bellman and Graham Spencer, the new Diving Supervisor on the *Star Hercules,* were chuckling playfully at Brian's discomfort. Graham's amusement was heightened by visual evidence of the attacks on his blurry monitor. Even Charles 'The Colonel' Raynor, who had chosen to base himself on the dive vessel, after the string of unwelcome incidents which saw Richard moved on and could affect the tendering on imminent operating licences, was also amused by the grief caused. He was hovering around impatiently with his hands in his pockets, behind his seated supervisor.

"Not much I can do from here, Diver One," Graham added unsympathetically, managing not to laugh.

"Magic. Thanks."

The attacks could only be defended with a gloved fist or glancing elbow if they were launched in the pale light cast around by the bell or narrow beam of his torch. In complete darkness at two hundred and ninety metres underwater, only ten short of the equivalent height of the Eiffel Tower's viewing platform, he had never felt more alone. Occasional spurts of defensive bioluminescence in the dark were the only clue to the location of the fish's most recent predation.

"OK, Topside. Valve now fitted and opened. Heading back to the bell, hope Jaws doesn't get me on the way."

Graham reassured his diver sarcastically, "You have your torch, Diver One. You'll be fine!"

After what must have been a record time for swapping a well-head valve, a perturbed Brian reached the bell and received little sympathy from his partner either. Brian still had his hair on shaggy winter setting while Malcolm's head had been shaved in the heat of the southern hemisphere summer. Looking like a kiwi fruit with a moustache, Malcolm mocked the bravery of Diver One while pulling him into the bell.

"Bloody wimp! I should have bloody gone out there. I could have done my party trick," he said, while throwing his eyes at the harpoon gun he always brought into the bell.

"OK boys. Close the door and we can start lifting the bell and you can go straight into decompression. Thanks for the last four weeks and a great dive today, Diver One." Graham said through the bell speaker. But before decompression commenced they had to revisit the bell. The operating platform nearby radioed that the valve hadn't come online as expected and advised it should simply be closed and opened again.

"Sorry guys. I have some bad news for you. We have to send you back down for a quick job. That valve needs opening and closing again."

Such news would normally anger Brian, especially as it was the last dive of four weeks confinement, but he started to smile inanely at Malcolm instead and said with obvious relish, "Your turn to take on Jaws then, Malc!"

"No problem!" While the bell was nearing the seabed again so soon after it had just left, Malcolm fitted his helmet. Through his microphone, he instructed Brian the Bellman, "When I'm just out of the bell, when I put my hand up can you pass me my harpoon?"

Brian nodded while still grinning as he handed Malcolm his weapon so he could finally perform his much spoken of party piece. Malcolm dropped off the stage to the disturbed seabed and headed for the valve in question. He closed it and re-opened it and confirmed as much to topside before gripping the handle of his harpoon gun with his right hand and resting the stock in his left palm, ready for action like a Hollywood hero.

"Topside, this is Diver One. Valve closed and reopened. Now I'm gonna take care of this monster," Malcolm said of his impending session of saturation angling.

"OK Diver One. Thanks and good luck with the creature of the deep."

Right on cue, a fish fitting Brian's description became visible in the beam of his torchlight. After striking against every other fish in the vicinity, Malcolm watched it turn and head straight at him. There was no time after he took aim to actually fire the harpoon, so the fish bayonetted itself in between its maniacal eyes. Then Malcolm fired, sending the tail of the harpoon deep into the body, with only a cord visible at the entry point. It writhed and twitched but the barbed harpoon was embedded, Malcolm just had to hang on until it lost its fight.

It made for a triumphant and no less heroic return as Brian and Malcolm pulled the ugly beast up into the bell. Brian identified it as the same one that had been launching itself at him. But, impressed as he was with Malcolm's courage, he had one question for his partner.

"Great trick and all, but what the fuck are we going to do with it?"

"We can give it to the galley and we can eat the bastard! Some English fish and chips, eh?"

"But it won't fit through the airlock. It's bloody massive."

"We'll have to cut it up into smaller bits."

"With our diving knives? In the chamber? That will be honking in there after a few days."

But Malcolm already had the solution, "We can do it in the wet room and wash it out after. Stop being a wimp, Brian! What do we care, we are out of here now anyway?"

Malcolm was right. The wellhead valve was now in operation and the still unidentified species was butchered and squeezed through to the galley, coating the tubular airlock with coagulating blood and fish guts. The decompression, the tedious gradual rise to the surface, began in earnest back in the living quarters. They were rising at roughly thirty metres every twenty-four hours, in terms of pressure in the chamber. The last ten metres were the most critical of all and where most issues become palpable. So nine days of tedium awaited them, not accounting for any problems, which would inevitably lengthen this timeframe.

And there were problems.

Brian was aware that the decompression chart in use was a modified U.S. Navy table, with no scheduled rest stops. Equalising stops are necessary for two reasons. Firstly, they allow the body a break from the constant shift of gases saturated in the bloodstream towards the lungs to dissipate. Secondly, it was important that the diver was always conscious while decompressing and able to report bend-like symptoms should they arise, so the rest stops allowed for some sleep.

"Can we put a couple of rest-stops in decom chart, please," Brian asked, as he was dependent on the crew at that stage as any other, until the chamber door finally opened.

"We'll see it gets done," Graham replied keenly before Charles silently overruled his diving supervisor with a tap on his shoulder and shake of his head while mouthing the words, "we don't have time, bud."

At roughly one hundred metres, six days into decompression, Malcolm developed a pain in his left knee and the decompression was paused while the ache was diagnosed as a 'pain-only' decompression sickness by the onboard Brazilian doctor, Dr. Edson Silva. Graham partially increased the pressure in the chamber as Malcolm breathed a higher concentration of oxygen through a face mask, with the aim of relieving the uncomfortable symptom. The pulsing in his knee subsided and decompression recommenced under the guidance of Graham and a worried Charles, who was pacing up and down the control room of the *Star Hercules*.

Two days passed before a far bigger problem was reported, just nineteen metres off the surface and freedom. Brian was playing a game of backgammon with Malcolm and discussing their mutual experience of sharing a chamber with Red Mist Ron: "Yeah, that Ron was a fucking loon. He looked like he was just a medication adjustment away from a meltdown."

At this point, Brian became disorientated. He stood up at the very moment a drop in pressure occurred corresponding to a one and a half metre drop on the decompression charts: he initially dismissed it as movement of the shipment. Then overwhelming nausea and tunnel vision swiftly followed. He lifted his head to see Malcolm had slumped back uneasily into his bunk. His expression was glazed and his left side was paralysed. Jumbled and dizzy, Brian pushed the call button and managed to say "STOP!"

Despite Charles's having chosen Graham was mostly on the grounds of his character of a compliant arse-kisser, he at least knew to recompress the chamber in two stages, down to forty metres where they were held. Brian grabbed the oxygen bib on the third weary grab at it and pulled the strap back over his cranium, his hairs pulling painfully against the dry perished rubber. As his head cleared his proprioception improved and then he fitted the second bib over Malcolm's blank face. They were both fed a 50/50 mix of helium and oxygen for the following twenty-four hours. The poorly maintained workings of the *Star Hercules* had been feeding false readings of the oxygen pressure in the chamber to the new Supervisor's control panel. His two divers had been consuming too much oxygen which had promptly brought on more dizziness and stupefaction, effects of oxygen narcosis. Much more of that and they both would start have started fitting.

As the oxygen was corrected to more therapeutic levels, Charles was in state of panic about losing his job and had contacted the Hyperbaric Centre in Aberdeen from the ship. He passed on their medical advice to Graham. However, while Brian was conducting skin tests to determine whether his dive partner had recovered sufficiently to continue decompressing, Charles Raynor and Dr. Edison Silva were leaving the *Star Hercules* on the helicopter that had just carried the on-shore doctor aboard. The pair spent the most critical stages of decompression of two divers in their care, who had both suffered incidents capable of causing permanent disability or death, bar hopping around Copacabana beach sinking Malibu.

Malcolm's prognosis from the tests of an 85% recovery was deemed enough to bring them up again. Brian's dive buddy was the priority and in the panic to recompress he blamed the excess oxygen present in the chamber for his own episode. But as the pressure dropped, the dizzy blindness returned. Only ten metres below the surface, Brian stumbled, shook his head to clear whatever was clouding it, then slumped between the two shallow bunks. Weakened by his own semi-paralysis, Malcolm was slow to pull himself from his bunk onto his unsteady feet. Brian heard him push the call button and return the favour of shouting "STOP!". He also remembered the coldness of the tread-plate floor, which his sweaty forehead felt glued to and was comforting at least.

He could decipher the hiss of gas entering the chamber, taking them deeper once again and prolonging their exit. But he couldn't respond to any of Malcolm's questions.

Nor could he move his limbs to aid his partner's attempts at lifting him. All he could manage was to do was to breathe and blink. Having signed up to fulfill a contract in Brazil he never should have, and after pulling his dead friend from the wreckage of a helicopter he could so easily have been on himself, was this Brian's own involuntary exit out of commercial diving?

19. Report

Brian woke up in his bed in Cabo Frio the first morning after decompression had ended, more grateful than ever to have the privilege. To hear the waves through his open window before he even opened his eyes, the ring of buzzing insects enlivened by the sunrise, were never more pleasing. He knew he was lucky to be tucked under his satin sheets and not in a wheelchair. His brain however felt burned and pounded behind his eyes, but he could still walk, talk and had retained all ten fingers, just. He had just dodged disaster with the series of mishaps in the lead up to his decompression sickness. Brian could feel time being called on his career, and the clock was ticking louder and louder.

```
10-OCT-83 12:14
TELEX. NO. 804
FROM: LONDON HYPERBARIC MEDICAL SERVICE.
TO: MARSAT INTERNATIONAL.
ATTEN: CHARLES RAYNOR
DATE: 10.10.83


MEDICAL REPORT ON BRIAN WORLEY


DEAR SIRS,
```

SALVAMAR – A TALE OF SALVAGE & DEEP DIVING

RE: BRIAN MICHAEL JOHN WORLEY DOB: 14.08.1942

I EXAMINED THIS MAN ON 6TH FEBRUARY 1983 AT 144 HARLEY STREET, LONDON, W1 FOLLOWING A DECOMPRESSION SICKNESS INCIDENT OCCURRING ON THE 28TH JANUARY WHILE BEING DECOMPRESSED FROM SATURATION.

HE AND HIS COLLEAGUE HAD BEEN STORED AT 950 FSW AND WERE BEING DECOMPRESSED ON A MODIFIED TABLE FROM WHICH THE CUSTOMARY STOPS FOR REST HAD BEEN LEFT OUT. DURING THE LATTER PART OF THE DECOMPRESSION, WORLEY'S PARTNER HAD A KNEE BEND. FULL RELIEF WAS OBTAINED BY CYCLES OF INCREASED OXYGEN BREATHING (THE NORMAL PARTIAL PRESSURE OF OXYGEN DURING THE DECOMPRESSION WAS 600 MILLIBARS).

THE PARTNER, (MALCOLM FERGUSON) LATER COMPLAINED OF NUMBNESS IN HIS LEFT SIDE AFFECTING MAINLY HIS ARM AND FACE. AT 57 FSW, WORLEY DEVELOPED TUNNEL VISION, NAUSEA, DIZZINESS AND COLLAPSED. HE ASKED FOR THE DECOMPRESSION TO BE STOPPED. THIS WAS DONE. HIS COLLEAGUE

WAS SIMILARLY AFFECTED AND THEY WERE RECOMPRESSED 134 FSW. FOLLOWING SOME CYCLES OF INCREASED OXYGEN BREATHING THEY WERE DECOMPRESSED IN THE PREVIOUS MANNER AND LEFT THE CHAMBER FREE OF SYMPTOMS.

AT THIS INITIAL EXAMINATION NINE DAYS AFTER THE INCIDENT HE COMPLAINED OF DIFFICULTY THINKING, HEADACHES WHICH HE DESCRIBED AS "SPONGY", SHORTNESS OF TEMPER AND COULD NOT BE BOTHERED WITH ANYTHING. HIS SPEECH WAS FREQUENTLY SLURRED AND HE WAS FORGETFUL, LOSING THE TRAIN OF HIS THOUGHT QUITE SUDDENLY AND FREQUENTLY.

GENERAL PHYSICAL EXAMINATION REVEALED NO GROSS ABNORMALITY, INDEED BUT FOR CEREBRAL SYMPTOMS DESCRIBED ABOVE HE WAS IN GOOD PHYSICAL CONDITION AND I FELT THAT WITHOUT THESE SYMPTOMS IT WOULD BE PROPER TO LET HIM RETURN TO FULL DIVING DUTIES WITHIN A MONTH AS IS NORMAL BRITISH PRACTICE.

I ADVISED HIM INITIALLY THAT SINCE HE HAD AN APPARENTLY APPROPRIATE TREATMENT

THEN A QUIET LIFE WITH PLENTY OF REST WOULD BE OF BENEFIT AND I WOULD REVIEW HIM AFTER A PERIOD OF SIX OR EIGHT WEEKS. SHOULD HIS PROBLEMS RECUR, THEN I WOULD DISCUSS THEM WITH SURGEON COMMANDER DAVID LEITCH OF THE ROYAL NAVY INSTITUTE OF NAVAL MEDICINE. HE HAD ALREADY BEEN INVOLVED AND HIS VIEW, LIKE MINE WAS THAT CEREBRAL SYMPTOMS STILL PERSISTED, BUT IN VIEW OF THE LONG TIME SINCE THE INCIDENT IT WAS UNLIKELY THAT ANY BENEFIT WOULD BE OBTAINED BY RECOMPRESSION OR BY FUTURE OXYGEN BREATHING WITH OR WITHOUT PRESSURE.

I REVIEWED MR WORLEY AGAIN ON 10TH MARCH. THE PHYSICAL STATE WAS UNCHANGED. PSYCHO-NEUROLOGICAL TESTS OF A SIMPLE NATURE SHOWED CONSIDERABLE DEFICIT IN SHORT AND LONG TERM MEMORY, WITH HESITANCE AND DIMINUATION OF PSYCHOMOTOR SKILLS AND SUPPRESSION OF INTELLECTUAL FUNCTION.

I REQUESTED A FORMAL REVIEW BY CONSULTANT NEUROLOGIST, DR K.J. ZILKHA OF THE NATIONAL HOSPITAL FOR NERVOUS DISEASES, QUEEN SQUARE, LONDON. HIS

OPINION WAS THAT THERE WAS NO GROSS OR
LOCALIZED LESION, BUT DIFFUSE DAMAGE OF
A MINOR NATURE WAS PRESENT THROUGHOUT
THE CORTICAL REGIONS AND SOME RECOVERY
COULD BE EXPECTED. A CT SCAN SHOWED NO
SIGNS OF INTRACRANIAL LESION OR ANY
AREAS OF SCARRING.

AT THIS TIME IT WAS FELT THAT SOME
ADDITIONAL BENEFIT MIGHT BE HAD FROM
SOME HYPERBARIC OXYGEN. A TWO WEEK
COURSE OF TREATMENT WAS THEREFORE
ARRANGED, BREATHING OXYGEN FOR 90
MINUTES AT 30 FSW ONCE A DAY. MR WORLEY
FELT SOME OVERALL IMPROVEMENT WAS
OBTAINED. MAINLY HIS MEMORY AND
INTELLECTUAL FUNCTIONS WERE BETTER.
THERE WAS ALSO A REDUCTION IN THE
FREQUENCY OF HIS HEADACHES.

OVER THE NEXT THREE MONTHS A SLOW BUT
STEADY IMPROVEMENT WAS MAINTAINED AND
FELT HE HAD MADE A FULL RECOVERY WITH NO
OBVIOUS IMPAIRMENT, THE HEADACHES HAD
CEASED AND HE HAD A SENSE OF WELL BEING.

HE HAS MOREOVER CONTINUED TO KEEP ME
INFORMED OF HIS PROGRESS BY LETTER AND

TELEPHONE CALLS. IT IS CLEAR THAT HE IS CONTINUING TO SUFFER ATTACKS OF HEADACHES AND CEREBRAL MALAISE WITH NO PRECIPITATING CAUSE.

OPINION

THIS MAN HAS SUFFERED A SEVERE CENTRAL NERVOUS SYSTEM DECOMPRESSION SICKNESS ON 28TH JANUARY 1983. THE DAMAGE IS ALMOST ALL CEREBRAL. DIFFUSE AND IN THE AREAS OF BRAIN NOT NOTED FOR DRAMATIC SYMPTOMS. DESPITE THE APPARENT SUCCESS OF THE ORIGINAL TREATMENT IT IS CLEAR THAT FULL RELIEF WAS NOT OBTAINED, BOTH THE ORIGINAL DECOMPRESSION TABLES AND THE THERAPEUTIC REGIME ARE SUSPECT.

THE APPARENT FULL RECOVERY OF FUNCTION IS IN PART DUE TO THE REDUCTION OF SWELLING THAT TAKES PLACE DURING THE BRAIN SCARRING, THE REMAINDER IS DUE TO BRAIN'S ABILITY TO USE ALTERNATIVE PATHWAYS THROUGH UNDAMAGED AREAS TO REPLACE THE LOST FUNCTION. IT IS LIKELY HOWEVER THAT MORE DETAILED PSYCHOLOGICAL TESTING WILL SHOW SEVERE DEFICITS.

MR WORLEY IS PHYSICALLY FIT TO DIVE
AGAIN BUT MENTALLY, AS A RESULT OF THIS
INJURY I WOULD STRONGLY ADVISE AGAINST
ANY FURTHER DIVING HE HAS HAD A SERIOUS
DECOMPRESSION INCIDENT FROM WHICH HE DID
NOT RECOVER FULLY DURING THE INITIAL
TREATMENT.

ASSESSMENT OF THE CORRESPONDENCE WHICH
CONTINUES TO ARRIVE FROM HIM INDICATES
THAT THE INJURY HAS RESULTED IN CEREBRAL
DAMAGE CAUSING INTERMITTENT BEHAVIOURAL
DISTURBANCE WITH MARKED SWINGS IN MOOD
AND AFFECT. MY PREVIOUS PROFESSIONAL
KNOWLEDGE OF HIM GOING BACK TO 1977
SHOWS THAT THIS IS A DEFINITE AND
PERMANENT CHANGE.

DESPITE THE INJURY I REGARD HIM AS FIT
TO DISCHARGE ALL TOPSIDE DUTIES RELATED
TO DIVING AND OFFSHORE WORK GENERALLY.

DR. JOHN D. KING

MD, BS, LRCP, MRACS, AFOM.
SPECIALIST IN OCCUPATIONAL HEALTH.
SPECIALIST IN HYPERBARIC MEDICINE.

SALVAMAR – A TALE OF SALVAGE & DEEP DIVING

MEDICAL DIRECTOR, LONDON HYPERBARIC
MEDICAL SERVICE

COULD YOU PLEASE ACKNOWLEDGE RECEIPT OF
THE ABOVE TELEX. THANK YOU

And with that, Brian's lengthy subsea career was over, brought to an inevitable close by the telex machine of Dr. John King. Another victim of decompression sickness or the 'Divers Disease'. It was a grim read for Brian, though not a surprising one. And the changes in character had indeed been swift. Gone was the affable, laid-back temperament, replaced by rage and anger. This was further exacerbated by the way Marsat had treated him after the incident, which only served to deepen his resolve. Confusion replaced certainty, and a bleariness succeeded his normal brash blasé manner. He suffered from frequent blank spots and debilitating migraines that could last for days, while his memory could no longer be relied upon.

Following his examination in London, he returned to Brazil to pursue a case of negligence against Marsat, Rio being closer to the location of the incident and the legal case had to be pursued in Brazil. It was also cheaper and sunnier than Brighton at that time of year, or Cassis, which was in the grip of bitter mistral winds whistling down off the Alps. Marsat had frozen wage payments to Brian after the accident, leaving him to fend for himself financially. He intended to lodge a case of negligence against Marsat, wholly represented on the *Star Hercules* by Charles Raynor and Dr. Edison Silva. He would challenge them to produce certificates or evidence of professional training in Hyperbaric Life Support and qualifications to practice Hyperbaric Medicine respectively. That they abandoned ship with two divers having suffered decompression events would provide any court, Brazilian or otherwise, with a lowly character reference of both defendants. A former diving colleague had offered to corroborate Brian's case by providing statements regarding a previous instance of willful neglect on Charles Raynor's part, the reason for 'The Colonel's' enforced relocation to Brazil in 1979.

It was an episode with many parallels to Brian and Malcolm's case: it was claimed that Raynor had again left a dive vessel with divers still held under pressure. Having arrived in the sound port of Haugesund in Norway, he told the divers they were having a twelve-hour rest stop, then disembarked with the crew to the local bars, leaving only a diesel mechanic behind on the ship. On discovery, Raynor was dismissed with immediate effect. In the same way that Brian had bent the truth about his date of birth, Raynor had found a way to be back in work in Brazil two months later. In addition to his statement of facts and copies of company records, Brian's former colleague could bear witness to the character of Charles Raynor.

In the melee that followed Malcolm's and Brian's eventual arrival on the surface, Malcolm had had the presence of mind to tear off the decompression schedule hanging out of the dot-matrix printer, fold it and slid inside his duffel bag. Brian was due to collect his scheduled flight ticket back to the UK, but no responsible person was present in the office in Rio to meet Brian to manage or even acknowledge the incident. As he was only concerned with the legal case and with no immediate plans to work again, Brian returned to Brazil. Years of living in the sun made winters of any form unpalatable and something to be avoided at all costs. Before his last hitch in saturation, Brian had been having thoughts of settling in Brazil after his diving career ended.

He had to reel in his outgoings while he was without an income and the first toy up for sale was *Highroller*, which had only recently seized back from the clutches of Spanish authorities. It was sold by a local agent to a Gibraltarian. The planned Morocco and Mauritania salvage jobs were then let go: with no income and without a boat he couldn't oversee the job or transport divers around from site to site and would lose his financial collateral in the deal. Hemorrhaging cash, he further reduced his outgoings by laying off Lolly, who had been on winter retainer payments to remain in Brighton and do anything locally thrown up by the *Dalhousie* project.

"Bri-yon, you have sacked Lolly?" Anne asked over the crackly phone line from Marseille.

"Yeah, sorry Anne. Things aren't going too well at the moment."

"You don't sound yourself, Bri-yon. Is everything OK with you?"

"Had a bit of problem down here last time, Anne."

Anne could tell that whatever was troubling Brian, he wasn't ready to discuss it. "OK Bri-yon, tell me when you are ready. By the way, your landlord in Cassis has been ringing me, you are three months behind with the rent. You are going to lose that apartment, Bri-yon."

"Only three? Oh, well," he wistfully replied.

"But Bri-yon, you'll lose all your things in there," she paused as each possession of value in Brian's Cassis flat came to mind. All of which was of no worth to Brian. "Your beautiful cashmere sweaters, your cameras, your coffee machine, that cost a fortune!"

"It doesn't matter, Anne. I have to stay here for a bit longer."

All the supporting evidence relevant to the case was combined by Brian's Brazilian lawyer; dive records, decompression chart and the print out, medical report, Brian's translated statement, loss of contracted and potential earnings. Given Marsat's conduct and that of their appointed Saturation Manager and doctor before, during and after an incident that had ended the careers of both divers, there would only be one outcome. It was only a matter of exactly how much it would cost them.

20. Comando Vermelho

A court date was set for Thursday 5th November 1984 at an unpronounceable court building in downtown Rio. So Brian had six months to kill in Brazil. He planned on spending most of it lolling around the beach in his swimming trunks, in the name of recovery. He had reconciled with himself to retirement from diving and along with it, bid farewell to the fear and risks, ear infections, killer fish, bad gas and living for four weeks at a time with social miscreants like Red Mist Ron. But his legacy of headaches, blank spots, lethargy and rages persisted. Every day the effects were different, but he applied a simple treatment; when he felt unwell, he stayed at home and drank cups of tea, sometimes for days at a time. On better days, when he sensed his energy levels were back to normal, he went exploring – around Rio and even into the Amazon rainforest on an off-road motorcycle.

He hadn't completely abandoned his plans of living in Brazil though, not for the first time, he was struggling with language lessons. His French was laughable given how much time he had spent in Cassis, but Brazilian Portuguese was an unintelligible struggle, one which he fruitlessly pursued when able, with infrequent classes and a course of cassette tapes. He may have been a good saturation diver but he was never going to be a linguist. It is said that when a language is spoken poorly it is being 'murdered'. Whenever Brian attempted some French or Portuguese, he was sneaking up behind the language in a dark alley and slitting its throat.

SALVAMAR – A TALE OF SALVAGE & DEEP DIVING

If he was to stay in South America, regardless of the outcome of the court case and speaking only pidgin Portuguese, Brian would eventually need an income. He tried and failed to bring a TV documentary production company in for a motorbike safari of the Amazon, to film a two-wheeled trek through the dense and largely unknown habitat. A further uncommissioned proposal was to fix another documentary film about the tremendous amount of year-round samba schools in Rio that enter the February carnival. Schools that were packed with gyrating dancers performing a dance that looked like upright intercourse, set to music.

One notion that appeared to get more traction was his plan to interview an infamous British resident of Rio: the bête noire of British establishment for nineteen years, an un-extraditable thorn in the sides of successive governments, Great Train robber Ronnie Biggs. 'The Great Train Robbery' in 1963 was still regarded as the crime of the century, Ronnie Biggs had been imprisoned in 1964 for his part in the heist. He escaped a year later, first to Paris for plastic surgery, then on to Australia and eventually Brazil. They had met as members of the Rio ex-pat community and shared an affinity having both grown up in East London. Always mixing socially in a felonious crowd, Ronnie was less inclined to do paid interviews given the recent success his son had been experiencing. In a bizarre quirk of fate, his six-year-old son had gained national publicity through appealing for the safe return of his father who had been kidnapped by bounty hunters. Within a couple of years, his son Michael was the lead singer in Brazil's biggest boy band, The Magic Balloon Gang. Prior to his son's success, Ronnie had been doing paid TV and press interviews and even sang vocals on two Sex Pistols singles.

"So I had friends here who said come down. They said there were 100,000 Nazis in the area after World War Two, so no one was gonna dig me out 'ere." Ronnie explained, his coiled silver hair, bulging cheekbones and rakish blue eyes forever moving to emphasise his speech.

"So why do other interviews in the past, Ron?" Brian asked.

"Simple, Brian. I needed the fucking money. The robbery money ran out before I left Australia for 'ere."

"Think about it though, Ron. We could do a positive take on you. Show the human side, not the celebrity bullshit. You never know, it might change how people perceive you back home," Brian knew Ronnie missed his home country and wasn't shy of using it as a negotiation tool.

"I'll think about it Brian. Sounds interesting though."

The court date arrived with Brian wearing a suit for the first time in years. The limited selection in the suit hire shop in Cabo Frio reduced his choice down to a shiny coffee coloured, double breasted chalk-stripe outfit. The glossy stripe running down the outside seam of each trouser leg gave the appearance of a cruise ship compère. On the steps leading up to the courthouse, in the shade of palm trees, Brian's lawyer shook his client's hand and mockingly viewed his suit. But Brian needn't have bothered. There would be no court hearing. Both Charles Raynor and Dr. Silva had declined to give evidence. Both kept their jobs, since removing them from their respective posts would serve as acknowledgement the accident had taken place. With the operating licence in its final year and negotiations at an early stage for a renewal, Marsat had to appear whiter than white. So the company lawyer had been summarily dispatched downtown to the court building. In a clammy corridor by the entrance of the assigned court, among the great and good of Rio, a podgy-faced American man approached, with heavily slicked hair and a dandruff covered suit every bit as awful as Brian's.

"Are you Mr. Worley?"

"Yes."

"I'm Miles Kniep, Marsat's legal representative for Latin America," Miles correctly guessed the tall man stood next to Brian was his lawyer and addressed them both with the nonchalance normally reserved for when buying a newspaper. "I'm here to settle out of court with you." Miles released the tight hold on the shoulder strap of a soft leather tote bag, which had been constant in such insalubrious surroundings and passed it to Brian. "I think you'll find that a royal offer, Mr. Worley. The settlement agreement is on the top in there."

Brian pulled at the zip, revealing its contents of cash and some paperwork. He handed the agreement to his lawyer as they all stood in awkward silence. Brian visually reckoned the amount with his jaw jutting before his lawyer handed his client the contract back to sign while nodding approvingly with pursed lips. As Brian signed the agreement against the tiled corridor wall, Miles gave him a verbal overview of the outcomes. "This relieves Marsat from any responsibilities towards your health or disability, signs away your right to enact future legal proceedings against Marsat and the amount $50,000 dollars US is offered as a full and final payment, in light of both unpaid and future earnings."

Within an hour of greeting each other on the court steps, Brian was again shaking his lawyer's hand beneath the palm trees before they parted for a final time. He stood there alone for a brief moment before hailing a taxi back to Cabo Frio as he didn't want to trust the security on public transport, Brian loosened his terrible tie and said to himself, "Magic!"

Safely back in his apartment and confined there by a violent storm that also emptied the beach below his balcony, he poured a large cognac, lit a cigarette and sat staring at the booty. He would have to invest it for his future as there would be no more easy and substantial pay cheques from diving. He mused on the possibilities the payout gave him. It was too late to rekindle the Morocco and Mauritania salvage jobs, which had been assumed by others in the meantime. For all his efforts, he would still need an income outside of diving to sustain him once it all came to an end. The *Dalhousie* project could get a cash boost, to get that over the line and act as a leader for other salvage projects. And what about staying in Brazil? He still was hopeless with Portuguese but $50,000 was understood and gladly accepted in any language. Maybe he could buy a quiet beach bar tucked in a lazy cove and see out his days in sandals and shorts, to the sound of the waves breaking on the shore. Before his thoughts could run too far ahead of himself, he received a pretty decisive phone call. A sinister voice, thick with a Brazilian accent spoke down the line, Brian's chin jutted out further as the call went on.

"Meet me at Banco de Brasília in Cabo Frio at 11 o'clock tomorrow morning. We have the money paid to us first yes? Then we take 10% and we transfer the rest to your account. If you don't do that, you won't leave the country alive. Nice evening." Then the line went dead. As polite as the surprise caller had been, the ominous advice was scarcely disguised as a question, rather than the order it actually was. Whoever it was, if they had Brian's phone number, then it was likely they knew his address also. It seemed that Charles Raynor, who was hindered by the limitations of tendering politics when it came to wreaking revenge on his accuser, had sought redress by other means. He had crossed paths with enough figures in the organized crime world through association with a corrupt local and national government to have got to know one or two of them. And now one was threatening Brian and doing a convincing job of it. Suddenly the prospect of a return home to the UK seemed much more palatable and his fondness for Brazil weakened.

Luckily Brian had made note of his appointment as he woke the following morning with a blank and pulsating head, a painful reminder of why $50,000 dollars was parked on his glass dining table. He arrived at eleven o'clock and rightly guessed his suitor was the man standing outside the branch wearing a blue suit, mirror sunglasses and chewing an unburnt match like a cowboy. His advisor on financial matters explained during a disjointed Anglo-Latin conversation that the $50,000 would be deposited into his 'organisation's' account for twenty-four hours, to which a 10% surcharge would be applied before it was transferred into Brian's local account. In a reversal of the day before, he left the bank $50,000 down, again squinting with confusion and fear that he would never see the payout again. Easy come, easy go.

All he could think of doing for twenty-four hours was to pack what he could into whatever suitcases he had, ready to bolt to the airport the following day, with or without the money. He took a final evening walk along the white beach at Cabo Frio, a place he had long thought he would stay. He stopped occasionally to sit on the crude timber benches dotted along the base of the dunes at the back of the beach. He'd only managed to pack a fraction of what was in his apartment, once again closing the door on a home full of his belongings. And if Anne knew, she would be as furious with him as she had been with his forfeiting of his apartment and possessions in Cassis.

The gangster proved to be a man of his Portuguese word and at midday on 7th April, Brian anxiously emptied his account balance of $45,000 dollars into his tan briefcase. The taxi that had had brought him to the bank was waiting outside and heading for the airport next. No seats were available to London so he booked a ticket via Miami, where he could stop over for a few days with his friend Frank. They had met fifteen years before in Athens while both working for the entertainment services that were travelling around the American army bases in the Mediterranean. Frank's career had been as much of a Swiss army knife as Brian's; jazz drummer, comedian, erotic writer, chef and lastly, a two-time porn star. A relieved and increasingly drunk Brian whiled away a few days cruising the everglades on Frank's boat *Buddy's Baby*, drinking rum runner cocktails with his good friend.

21. Feeling Effects

126 Ferndene Road

London

SE24 0AA

15 November 1984

Dear Dr King

Enclosed please a find cheque for consultation 10th Sept. 84. Made out to the amount of £40.

I apologise for bothering you with my problem during your convalescence. Maybe I should book a bed beside you and we can compare notes. Unfortunately, the symptoms continued to persist and eventually I was forced to go to H.M.S. Vernon for therapeutic hyperbaric treatment daily as you recommended. I also had the CT brain scan at Cromwell Hospital and no doubt they will forward you the results in due course.

Hopefully the recompression treatment will bring some result as this situation is really getting me down. I hope to explain everything to you, as not only have you examined me regularly for physicals, but have known me personally over the years. For this reason, I don't have to tell you how this has affected me. I have waited a little while until the anxiety has worn off and can view the problem rationally. I try to honestly evaluate the symptoms remaining, attempting to isolate normal stress feeling.

I may begin to appear a little stupid or perhaps hysterical slightly. I don't know about the former but the latter is untrue. I'm just concerned by some recent effects and that they may have nothing whatsoever to do with my past symptoms. However, as they are fairly fresh in my mind I thought I would let you know, in case there is an answer somewhere.

I believe returning to the UK has been the best decision yet. It's quiet and out of the way, yet I'm close enough to the coast to keep in touch or visit when I feel like it.

At the present moment I'm just tidying up the paperwork and messing around with light equipment when I feel like it. Checking and cleaning camera equipment etc. Taking photos of cows and trees would you believe! If people who know me could see me,

I'm sure they would think I've gone off my chump. Seriously, I think I am on the right track and getting on top of the situation. But I cannot continue with this sedentary lifestyle indefinitely. Apart from the financial drain, I must think about my future.

To be honest, sometimes I don't know if it is just my imagination or temperament, as I know I'm getting tired of just sitting about. The only place I go when I feel up to it and can't face any more of my own cooking is the little Italian place around the corner.

I had to be sure the symptoms were not mixed up with possible frustration at giving up on the salvage projects overseas. I have been organising them for the past three years and obviously it's something you just don't let go and forget about.

I have been spending time cancelling arrangements and generally tidying up. Maybe I'll have another try some other time. At least with this off my mind I have been able to concentrate on real and actual symptoms and try to monitor myself daily.

First the headaches are still there and tightness over the eyes and slight pressure around the head. This I believe is the cause of the lack of concentration. When I speak for any length of time, or someone talks to me or I study something for too long the headache increases and in the end, that's all I'm thinking about. And I have to get away to somewhere quiet rather than continue to concentrate on what is being said or happening. I have difficulty in recognising even the most familiar things or equipment. I think the latter is only momentary because as I persist, I start doing things automatically and the feeling wears off. I have what can be best described as lapses in concentration – hardly worth mentioning on their own. Stupid things such as calling a taxi. Then for a moment, can't remember why I am waiting on the street. Walking past my front door or forgetting who I was about to telephone etc. I tried to read a book as a test and couldn't remember three lines.

So I still have loss of long and short term memory, and occasionally, false memories. Such as you think it is somebody's birthday on the wrong date or you think you have lost something around the house which you can't find, but it never existed in the first place.

I also have been suffering from a slight lack of coordination at odd times, that is taken for clumsiness. I have dropped a glass because I have either lost the feeling I was holding something or forgot! That time, people assumed I'd had too much to drink. Although I laughed it off, I resented this as I do not drink that much and only just been handed the glass of wine at a fairly formal garden party. I guess my personal embarrassment didn't help matters because thirty minutes later, I did it again.

Here in Brighton, I am able to go at my own pace. If I feel like doing something, I carry on until I don't feel like it. Then I either have to lie down or do something completely different. Physically I am still fit and sometimes get carried away feeling that I'm strong enough to shrug this feeling off. But in the end, I have to admit it beats me.

I am giving serious thought to giving up the offshore business for good. I have enjoyed the diving industry over the past fourteen years. It has given me a lot of independence and the thought of starting in a more sedentary lifestyle is a little depressing itself. With my normal functions impaired to such an extent, it is increasingly impossible to think of continuing in any position of responsibility in the diving industry. Mainly because, should an emergency arise, a decision of mine which could cause a situation I have experienced myself, would be totally wrong and I don't think I could handle the responsibility.
Therefore, I resigned myself to the fact it is time to give up the idea. Is it hard to accept as diving has

been a consuming interest. But in the long term, I honestly think it is the best decision I can make. Maybe sometime in the future, should I feel confident enough, perhaps I'll return to the business on a different level. But for the time being, my priority is to get on top of my current situation.

One incident was so clear in my mind I had to make notes in case I forgot the feeling. Last Friday, just after arriving back from Brazil, after spending a fairly relaxing week at home, I was on my way to Rayleigh in Essex to spend the weekend with my Mother. I had driven up from Brighton with plenty of time and was relaxed, the only thing on my mind was the weekend. I passed through the Dartford Tunnel and could remember sorting out small change to pay the toll. Just after leaving the tunnel I just suddenly went blank. I didn't know where I was, what side of the road I should be driving on, didn't recognise anything in the car (I have explained this to you before). The only way I can really explain the feeling is if you can imagine sitting next to a pilot in a plane and he suddenly disappears, leaving you in control!

I had traffic either side of me and did not know what to do and even what side to try to pull over. My reflexes were shot and I just sort of hung on to the steering wheel and tried to go in a straight line. You would have thought I had never been a car before in my life. Slowly the feeling cleared, but I was pretty shook up. Because of the traffic I couldn't pull over, but after a few more moments I somehow felt competent to carry on. No mad dash thereafter as you could imagine.

More like a pensioner out for a Sunday drive.

By the time I arrived at Rayleigh I felt OK. I haven't explained any of this to my Mother or any other family member mainly because she/they wouldn't understand and I have to drive myself crazy trying to explain. She thinks I am on extended leave. They are all used to my irregular times over the years so no problem really. I mention this because the conversation at home was normal and light, usual family gossip etc. I have a pretty relaxed family atmosphere. However, around four o'clock I felt the pressure around my head increase. I just couldn't bear to hear the television or any conversation. It was like my head was in a tin can. I had a lie down until eight o'clock. Although the main part of the headache had gone, my head still felt so tight and numb. Spongy is my best description.

Saturday, I had a headache for most of the day and I returned home on Sunday. From what I have noticed, I am pretty clear in the early morning (I like to get up around 6.30) especially around here. By midday I start to get tight and if I push myself, my head can feel as tight as a drum by the evening.

That's just about it I guess. The feeling on the road, I thought lasted for about 15 minutes. But looking back, I don't think it lasted that long and I can't really remember how far I travelled before it cleared off. I am keeping this problem from my immediate family for obvious reasons.

I sincerely hope you too are feeling better after your operation and I am sorry to have to bother you with

this problem at this time. But by
writing it, it also helps sort it
out for myself, in a way. Even if
doesn't help me come up with the
answers! There is no one here I can
talk to regarding all this. At least
I feel a little more assured by
being able to write about these
events and receive rational answers,
rather than this feeling that things
are getting away from me on
occasion.

Please forgive the long letter and
my babbling but I will continue to
keep you informed and once again,
thank you for your understanding and
assistance. Hope to hear from you
soon.

Best regards

Brian

22. Titanic

Brunswick Square in Brighton was dark and windy when Brian arrived. The gusts made his window frames creak and sheared what remained of expired summer foliage from the trees in the square. Around the base of each tree was a ring of gaunt rose bushes bravely nodding in the wind. The railing around the square was thick with leaves, collected and blown into place by the wintry gale. As the apartment slowly heated from its dank slumber, so the fusty atmosphere inside 26 Brunswick Place began to dry and Brian removed his leather coat. A restorative cup of tea and a cigarette followed. With every pane opaque with moisture, misty rain generated a gentle patter on the windows, before he switched on his Hi-Fi for some background music to fill the silence.

His elongated residence in Brazil meant that Brian had neglected to pay any rent to his furious landlord or the utility bills on his Brunswick penthouse. There was so much post waiting for him, it jammed under the door when he remembered the correct flat number and turned the key. Among the chorus of financial demands was notice of disconnection from his electricity provider, which had finally been enacted a week before his homecoming. So the first step into leading a more normal life was to run an illegal feed from his apartment into the junction box outside his front door, the electricity supply for the lift. With power and heating restored, he unpacked what possessions he had fled Rio with and five preserved piranhas he bought at the airport with the remaining Reals in his pocket. For his own health, he needed to put the events in Brazil behind him. The country had nearly killed him thrice. But the $45,000 was safe in his Jersey bank account. He recalled all the possessions he would prefer not to have left behind as he slowly emptied his luggage. Another wardrobe full of clothing, all his camera equipment, all the furniture: he had even left his car behind.

After the frightening drive to Essex which he recounted to his doctor, he became fearful of driving long distances and would try to avoid motorways for some time afterward. He was leaving the house less and less often, feeling nailed down by the moods that were a by-product of mapping new cerebral pathways in his brain. That and the frustration caused by the narrowing of his horizons owing to the repair work going on in his head. One development that did little to lift his temper was the discovery that the stern section of the *Dalhousie* was missing. It had been a year since Margaret Rule had inspected the finds. Despite its weight, it was suspected that gypsies, who had seized a nearby sports field around the time the stern vanished, had removed it and burnt off the wood for the non-ferrous yellow cladding and brass pins tying the structure together. So the sum of recovered articles from the *Dalhousie* was a compass bezel, mast-band, pintles, gudgeons and 8 irregular copper stakes. Scant return on all his outlay to prepare the barge and pay wages. Little more than could be recovered by a local diving enthusiast without the expense of chartering a barge or diving bells. When it came to any future funding with so few objects to titillate potential investors, only a madman would be investing in that project. After the publicity of the non-announcement, the wreck was no longer a secret either.

The bad news and change in climate combined to bring on a heavy cold, which he self-medicated with cups of sweet tea and glasses of hot red wine. He sorted out his affairs, cutting his losses wherever possible, forever aware not to overdo it mentally and bring on another crushing migraine. He also had to contemplate a land-based future, the playboy life having been curtailed after a very decent run. No more breathing Heliox, Hydrox, Nitrox or Trimix or god knows what else he had inhaled. It would just be a boring 20/80 oxygen/nitrogen mix in future. For the past fourteen years, even if he took time out for a few months, he always had a job to return to. A dive vessel waiting or an oil rig out there somewhere in the ocean. His cerebral condition had closed the door to that industry for him: it had been a signal it was time to leave the party.

The Maserati was the first major decision he needed to take, even if the long overdue repair bill had been reduced through the courts – he couldn't face spending another penny on it, after all the thousands that had been ploughed into the bloody thing. The paintwork wasn't designed to face a winter north of Modena, let alone five British ones in total, not including the balmy winters parked up in Marseille. The paintwork, which had been so impeccable and perfectly dark at the factory, was now either flat, fading to flat or the lacquer bubbling. Maybe it was evidence that his condition was actually affecting his judgement for the better, but the solution seemed simple: he gave the car keys to the mechanic and they were square and done.

He remained a riddle to himself and would forget he had bread in the toaster or was running a bath. Better days saw him at the gym or having a quiet dinner at Giuseppe's. Such days represented a return to his usual *joie de vivre,* to someone Brian could recognize in the mirror. Other days, when he rose with a heavy head, a conglomerate of anxiety and fuddled confusion, he would replicate the sleep patterns of a teenage sloth. Others might have diagnosed this as depression: he just felt helpless trapped in his own sluggish recovery and would rather not face another day if he had a choice. He didn't shave, listened to jazz and moved only from the sofa to kitchen and back, perhaps the bathroom at a push. The cream Trimphone on the dining table rang, but he didn't always pick up. It had phoned earlier that day, but Brian decided to answer this time.

"Am I speaking to Brian? Brian Worley?" asked a plummy voice.

"Yes I think so."

"My name is Ken. Ken Clutterbuck," Brian didn't recognize the name, so he let him continue. "I got your number from Terry the fisherman. I have a holiday home locally, you see. In Bexhill, just down the road to you."

"OK, hello Ken. What can I do for you?"

"I represent a consortium called Taurus International and we're just about to launch a survey project and we need your technical assistance."

"OK," Brian didn't want to sound thick, but he was keeping up with Ken.

"You have been working on the *Dalhousie*, have you not?"

"Yes that's true."

"How's that going, Brian."

"Nothing for the winter now. Maybe next year again." Which translated from the evasive bullshit it was, actually meant "Gypsies have stolen 90% of the finds for scrap money and I'm fucked!"

"Taurus International is based over in Paris and we require a salvage consultant to join our team?"

"Right?" Brian was slightly distracted as he grabbed around his messy dining table for a writing pad and pen to take notes.

"We have just lost an investor and are trying to save an expedition to survey the *Titanic*. We need to get you onboard to appeal for £2.2 million to keep the venture afloat, as it were!" On a consultant basis, there were few on the market as experienced as Brian: fate normally intervened before they could attain fourteen years of diving service. While he wasn't in a position to directly supervise any diving, his knowledge and expertise was of value to some.

"That sounds interesting, Ken. The holy grail of wrecks, eh?"

"Absolutely. Could you jump on the train to London tomorrow? Meet me in my office and we can discuss it further."

"I think I can, Ken. Yes!"

"There are several crews out there looking for the wreck as we speak, so it's a bit of a race against time. Hence the rush to speak to you. If we don't raise the money, then it will fall into American hands."

"We can't bloody have that can we, Ken!" Brian said, patriotically.

"And if you want to be more involved then you can buy into the project for £100,000."

"And what would a £100,000 get me if I did buy in?" Brian asked with his mandible out-stretched.

"A share of all profits from what we may salvage. We are in talks in regards to producing books and TV documentary about the finding of the ship."

"Hmm, OK. Something to consider."

"It's so close now. It could be huge, Brian. There are several crews out there looking forward, narrowing down the search for others like us, you know?"

"So hopefully you have timed it right?"

"Absolutely. Brian, I can brief you about the whole operation tomorrow but we have just secured the use of a titanium submersible capable of working at six thousand metres. What time would you be able to make it up here?"

"I could leave here after the daily rat race has finished in the morning. Say midday?"

"Great. We can do lunch then, sir?"

Brian was pleased the call had ended as the extra stimuli wasn't what the doctor ordered. His forehead had tightened during Ken's sales pitch. He had been pain-free all day until he replaced the receiver, but then the tightness grew to a dull pulsating thud above the bridge of his nose. He pulled his eyes shut, tighter and tighter after each clouding thump behind his pained forehead. A listlessness whisked him off to the chocolate chenille wool sofa, where he remained under a tartan blanket until the early hours. He wasn't really awake or asleep, just lost in his own confusion and discomfort, robbed of his usual energy.

Even if he didn't take up the chance to invest £100,000, which he didn't have anyway, he would be content to take a salary if it afforded a path out of the monotonous life he faced back on the beach. If Ken was to be believed, then it could be a springboard into more salvage consultancy for Brian. Not having lived in the UK himself for many years, Brian hadn't been aware of how many other similar interviews Ronnie Biggs had already done in the period before his son's success. There was little or no appetite in yet another review of the infamous and much raked-over past of an ageing villain. He was old news, despite his undoubted charisma and appeal to British celebrities visiting Rio, who were always eager to pose for a photo with the notorious Great Train Robber. And fixing it for a TV documentary crew to fly in from America and motorcycle through the Brazilian Amazon was impossible when you were based in Brighton. The *Dalhousie* salvage project was as good as dead too. The *Mount* barge was under a new charter and Lolly was back in France. Fitting out a new barge for a fresh attempt at salvaging what remained of the *Dalhousie* alone would consume most, if not all, of his pay-out.

23. Making Tracks

KEN - TAURUS - 01 5546732

LUNCH - 1200

LONDON

Brian was blank the next morning and had no recollection of the words and numbers that were written on a notepad next to the phone. A cigarette stirred nothing in his memory, neither did a cup of coffee. He speculated while showering, discounting early on the hypothesis that Taurus was Ken's star sign, but concluding that it must be an appointment of some kind. But where? And about what? Luckily he was able to dial the number and act dumb with Ken's receptionist, claiming he had mislaid the address details for their meeting later that day. The train journey up to London Victoria was a chastening experience of reintegration. All the sitting around involved in his recovery had been little preparation for the loud announcements, information boards, queueing to buy a return ticket and finding the right platform. His head was thankfully clear: he had taken two paracetamols as a precaution during his morning coffee, before his boiled eggs. The dreary mundanity of the people and their jaded passiveness made Brian fearful he would soon be living the same existence. He chose a dark grey suit with a white shirt and black tie from his full wardrobe and looked every bit as much the city gent as anyone else on that loud, jolting train. But he knew nothing of this life. Meanwhile his fellow commuters, if given the choice, would probably rather not live in a pressurised metal cylinder for weeks at a time, with daily trips to the bottom of the sea. Fourteen years out of the rat race made for an uneasy dip into normal life. Commercial diving had shown him the world, more than just the inside of an office or a train carriage.

He picked up an abandoned newspaper, a well-thumbed morning edition, from the empty seat next to him. He glazed over and looked at stories about the privatisation of British Telecom or the recording of the Band-Aid charity single. The train journey to London Victoria was only the half of it, as the underground tube network awaited him after that. Bond Street tube station the closest to Ken's office. It only involved a single switch from the Victoria to the Jubilee line at Green Park station, but Brian still managed to get the train running in the wrong direction at both stations.

Beneath a brass effect ceiling fan with three globe lightbulbs was Ken's desk, well ordered with a mocha leather writing pad in the centre. He clicked the spring action on an expensive looking pen as the two spoke. He was as posh as he had sounded on the phone, a portly, boyish face and had a pally nature in the flesh.

"So, let's pop out for some lunch, I know a nice spot around the corner. I have a journalist friend joining us who works for The Times. Thanks again for coming, by the way," Ken said bouncing on the balls of his feet as they were putting on their jackets before leaving his office.

Ken knew little about salvage and surveying, so Brian's experience in the team would be crucial. He evidently just knew how to make money. His journalist friend arrived after they had finished their steaks and the wine had started to flow. Brian had moved onto cognac by the time his picture was taken for the article. Ken continually emphasised the urgency of the venture and gave details of Taurus International, a French offshore project management company coordinating the venture. It's Paris-based chairman, one Robert Chappaz, was a friend of Ken's and the reason for his involvement. It was to be the first complete film survey of the famous ship, 74 years after it had sunk with the loss of over 1500 lives. There were lofty ideas of involving Prince Charles in the survey as an 'official observer' much like what had happened with the *Mary Rose*. The journalist and Brian scribbled notes as Ken explained the set-up: the journalist did so to pad out a piece for his newspaper and Brian because of his semi-amnesia.

"Basically we need to raise £2.2 million to save this expedition and we need the article for some publicity. The £100,00 buy-in is to get in 'on the ground' so to speak," Ken informed Brian, while releasing meat from between his teeth with a toothpick.

The return journey, back across London then on the train to Brighton, wasn't any more fun or less confusing. It set Brian thinking about a route out of normal life before it had even begun. Maybe it was bravado brought on by all the lunchtime alcohol, but Brian had a notion that he had the answer in his head somewhere. His offshore slush fund, once it was topped up with the Marsat pay-out, amounted to £65,000 in his bank in Jersey, £35,000 short of the buy-in figure. Money had only ever been numbers to Brian, numbers that, if played with shrewdly, would earn bigger numbers he could retire on. The well-developed deal-making, wheeling and dealing lobe of Brian's brain was obviously recovering at a rate in advance of his memory. By the time he was walking back across the foyer of Brighton station, through the aromas of cheap coffee and hot soup, he had convinced himself to review all the *Dalhousie* papers, including those added by Lolly's research before he reluctantly moved on to pastures French and new. While the thought was still alive, Brian made a note as there were no guarantees it would survive the night in his mind.

URGENT – LOOK UP DALHOUSIE STUFF

The scribble helped Brian solve the daily morning riddle of what had happened on the previous day. The file of papers about the *Dalhousie* was retrieved from his office in the second bedroom and dropped on the dining table in the bay window facing the sea. One cup of coffee wasn't enough to solicit what he was intending on finding in among the mass of papers. However, two more cigarettes and another coffee got things moving. The research by Lolly was in addition to all the previous investigation data. It appeared that he had been researching any clues to the missing inventory and into the previous conduct of the Captain, John Butterworth. Lolly had even managed to find the inventory of the *Dalhousie*'s former voyage from Calcutta, excitedly and entirely wrongly judging it to be that pertaining to the doomed passage. Each document felt like it was being viewed for the first time, which wasn't the case, but at least all the information he needed was there. Brian was confident he could piece it together given a day or two, which is really all the time he had to raise the £100,000. It was just a jigsaw, one consisting of hundreds of interlocking A4 size pieces.

Hours passed by as he sifted through every shred of paper, filtering out non-essential papers. Lolly had enough spare time while in Brian's employ to investigate the inventory of similar ships moving paid passengers to the new world for examples. It wouldn't fill in the *Dalhousie's* blank inventory, but it did provide an average of goods on other vessels. Ultimately though, it was a case of the passengers themselves; their wealth and status reflected in the goods they were transporting. Of the twelve passengers, Mr John Underwood bore the most scrutiny and was most likely the father of the family that had been washed off the capsized hull as they desperately offered their prayers up to the heavens. He intended on settling a business in Sydney, and as with the other passengers, travelled with all possessions of value from the 'old world'. Brian felt sure there must be something of value on that wreck, if it hadn't been removed in the meantime, following the announcement in the press of its discovery. The more he learnt, the faster his mind begun to spool. His hope overtook his brain's recent fondness for inventing things or wiping tracts of his memory.

Apart from his own life, there was nothing to lose and everything to gain. If he found nothing, there was a paid position waiting for him in the search for the *Titanic*. But Brian wanted a share and if he was right, his answer lay sixteen miles SSW from Beachy Head and forty metres down. According to his wreck layout diagram, a line could be drawn along the wreck from where stern section had settled, through the location of the mast band toward the remaining main anchor, which was still to be recovered, marking the bow of the *Dalhousie*. Towards the stern and on the same central bearing through the wreck rose a substantial mound, marked as a geological prominence over which the hull had slowly broken up.

Brian would need a trusty comrade in several crimes, one who was significantly better at navigating than him, and knew exactly who to phone. It rang three times before Bill answered in his usual jaunty fashion.

"Hello, this is the menswear department!"

"Hello Bill, you daft sod!"

"Hello Bri. How you doing, boy?"

"I'm doing OK, Bill."

"I was just saying to Pat yesterday that we hadn't heard from you in a while. Jesus, great to hear from you, pal."

"I've got a little adventure for you, Bill. If you're keen?"

"Blood-dy hell, yeah! Count me in, Bri. It is in this country?" Bill asked, thoroughly amused by the sudden reappearance of his daring friend.

"Yeah, it's the wreck I've been working on near Brighton. I've got something I have to check out."

"That sounds fun, Bri. I haven't been out there yet," Bill said, forgetting it had been three years since he first heard about the *Dalhousie*, on their gentle jaunt on *Highroller* down the Rhône to Marseille.

"When can you make it down, Bill?"

"I've got two more night shifts. Tonight and tomorrow. I normally get off a bit early on the last shift. Shall I drive down to you straight from there?"

"So that's tomorrow night. Sunday?" After a busy day, it was late afternoon and Brian was tiring.

"Well, Monday morning by the time I'm done, Bri. If I drive down after, I can get to your place about three in the morning I reckon."

"Magic, Bill. Should only be a few hours out there. I'll take you for a breakfast when were done, OK?" Brian wagered.

"Deal, Bri. Oh hang on, Pat just asked if you'll around for Christmas?"

"I hope so, Bill!" Brian joked. But Bill wasn't to know that was by no means certain if Brian dived again.

BILL - 3AM - MONDAY 10th DEC

24. Définitif Plongée

Brian slept very little for the following two nights, continuing to research the wreck and gathered equipment left around various locations from the *Dalhousie* works. By then he had entirely convinced himself about the fixation that had been sparked during the train ride back from London. Loaded in his car were three filled scuba tanks, two airlift bags, some metal rods, garden hand tools and a dark grey dry-suit. Under the weak light cast by a single incandescent bulb in his lounge, he inspected his diving helmet and torch on the walnut coffee table, glancing periodically at the clock, to note how long it was until Bill arrived. New batteries were fitted in each of the torches. He stayed awake on the Sunday night to run over everything, check then double check, and to make sure he didn't forget anything. He composed himself with the thought that he could cancel at any time and just take Bill for breakfast on the promenade. He could just sit there eating eggs and bacon, watching the dog walkers pass by and give up his life of risk and reward. But that was unlikely.

In the seamless calm of 3am, the night was truly soundless. No clunking lift outside his door, no traffic noise. Just the soothing hum of the city at rest. Alone with his thoughts and the gentle swash of the surf on Brighton's pebble beaches. Just minutes before Bill, who was rarely unpunctual, was due to arrive, Brian picked the phone. In a fatalistic flourish, he dialled Anne's number, just in case something went wrong over the next few hours. Only an hour ahead of British time, it rang once, a second time then her answering machine cut in.

When the cheery, but indecipherable message ended with a deafening beep, he took a breath and spoke;

"Hi Anne. It's Brian. I'm ringing to let you know I wanna take you up on your offer, if it still stands? That's all." If she had to wait another twenty years, she would always accept. Even if his memory was shot and failed often, he could never forget special Anne. By the time she heard the message later that morning, she phoned her husband-to-be back immediately, but there was no answer.

Bill progressed unhindered from Corringham to Brighton and arrived five minutes early, pressing Brian's intercom buzzer, which rang around the apartment.

"Morning sir. Give me two minutes and I'll be down. Saves you coming up."

"OK, Bri! I'll nip back to the car and grab the hood for my jacket. It's starting to rain."

As the entrance to the corner apartment block opened, five steps up from pavement level, Brian greeted his friend before walking towards his car. It was pre-packed with the necessities for their early morning adventure out into The Channel. They didn't notice the locksmith's van parked behind Brian's car, waiting to meet Brian's landlord to effect a repossession. During his recent mental malaise, Brian had neglected to respond to the many arrears demands, so the landlord had assumed his tenant was dead. Another abodes worth of belongings would soon be in the possession of an underpaid renter. Including his company-issue Comex Rolex, which lay unloved in the drawer of a bedside cabinet.

"Merry Christmas, by the way Bri."

"Yes, happy Christmas to you too." Brian grinned at Bill's infectious jollity. It was a tonic for his frequent gloom.

They caught up with each other on the journey along the coast to Newhaven, during which Bill noticed Brian's car had changed for the worse. The roads were glossy with drizzle under the amber street lights, while occasional flashing Christmas decorations offered an alternative to the orange tint. Foxes were the only road users at that hour.

"The beard suits you, Bri. Few grey hairs in there though," Bill ribbed.

"You've got a few too, I notice," Brian replied, deliberately looking at Bill's temples.

"Yeah I know, pal. But I've got two kids. What's your excuse?"

"God, don't ask!"

"So where's the Maserati, Bri?"

"Oh, I chopped it in. I had a huge repair bill and the paintwork basically dissolved."

"Shit, Bri."

"So I gave it to the mechanic. Was a bit of a baastard, but I had to wash my hands of it. But I did turn up there one evening to find they were closed, so I chucked a crankshaft I found in the yard through one of their windows."

"Beautiful thing, weren't she," Bill noted, using the maritime feminine. "This one's a bit slower, eh?"

"Yes, we'll have to wait until the summer to get a nought to sixty time as the days are longer," Brian joked. His dry humour had survived his personality changes. And he was deliberately trying to be his old self, to put on a show of normality for his friend.

"Bet you miss it, though Bri, eh?"

"How it looked and went, yes. The running costs, shit no."

They exited Newhaven Harbour at 3:20am, not in *Highroller* as Bill had expected. But in the small tender for the *Mount* barge, stolen or 'temporarily borrowed' for the occasion on account that it was the only thing left in the berth of the *Mount*, and obviously not part of its new chartering. The short-hulled rib-dinghy had a single outboard engine that Brian operated as Bill navigated by torchlight. Brian had removed his winter coat and pulled the dry-suit over his remaining clothes. Bill hadn't checked the hood for his ski jacket he pulled from the back seat of his car. His young son had a similar jacket, the removable hood for which Bill had picked up by mistake. Undeterred, he wore it as a stand-alone hood, even though it was as tight-fitting as a swimming cap and incapable of reaching and zipping into his upturned collar.

Once clear of the breakwater, on the fringes of The Channel, the dinghy began to dance and jump around, the small engine labouring. Captain Worley knew where they had to be, it was marked on the nautical charts and maps he had brought so that Chief Officer Hicks could decipher the way. They dodged the larger vessels forging the shipping lane, disorientating the navigator who was partially blinded by the glare of his slim torch, which he was holding in his mouth to free up both hands to hold a compass in one and the map in the other.

It was a mostly terrifying voyage of 40 minutes, sixteen miles SSW off Beachy Head, before they began circling to confirm Bill's certainty there were above the wreck, by finding the buoy. Bill switched off the torch and joined the search for any buoy-shaped abnormalities on the surface, while his eyes adjusted to the darkness. His first sight of land from their initial loop, brought home how far out they were.

"Blood-dy hell, Bri. Pat will bloody kill me if this boat goes belly up."

In the absurdity of the moment, Brian started laughing, "You silly sod. Oh hang on, I think I just saw something there, Bill."

Lady luck, who had been so absent on that night in October 1853, smiled on the daft pair. Brian immediately set the dinghy into reverse. On the horizon, the south coast of England was just a ribbon-thin belt of flickering golden lights, below cloud-like light pollution from inland. The beam from the lighthouse at Beachy Head pulsed with each revolution. Tying off on the buoy gave Bill no more sense of safety, though he comforted himself with the thought that at least getting back to shore wouldn't require a map.

Gambling against medical opinion, his own good sense and cerebral function, hyperbaric science and the advice of his friends and family (at least the advice they would have given if he had told them), Brian readied himself. He attached his weight belt to compensate for the spare scuba tanks, flippers and slid both his arms through the diving harness, lifting the primary cylinder onto his back. Bill could sense a hesitancy in his old friend, who was normally so cavalier. Brian hadn't dived for nearly two years and it was maybe a sign that his recovery wasn't near complete that he would even consider a nocturnal plunder on the wreck was a sound idea. Even more so as it came just after he had accepted a two-year old proposal. Bill started to feel more doubtful.

"Are you sure about this, Bri?"

"Sure as I can be."

"You wouldn't catch me going down there now, fuck that!" It was a statement most sane people wouldn't contest. "And what happens if you have a problem, Bri?"

Brian pushed out his lower jaw and shrugged. There was nothing Bill could do; Brian was on his own.

"Too blood-dy dangerous. But I guess you are used to hearing that."

"Yeah, I can't bloody wait until I finally drown so they realise how true it fucking is!" Brian joked as he lifted his helmet from his lap, over and onto his head. After connecting the tank to the helmet, he dropped backwards into the water. He surfaced and stared at the lighthouse in the distance, waiting for it to revolve one last time. He had visited the site many times, but never at night. He was in the same dark stretch of water at virtually the same time of morning as the sinking, 131 years earlier. The account of the sole survivor, Joseph Reed, was fresh in his unreliable mind: and it was an extremely disturbing memory given his circumstances. A bird's eye view of all those who perished that night.

Bill handed Brian the rods and hand tools, wrapped in the pair of air-lift bags. At 4:20am Brian pulled his head under the water. Perhaps the *Dalhousie* had unfinished business and would finally claim back the single, elusive life that survived the sinking. Bill traced the light from Brian's torch as it descended beneath the dinghy, a jade sphere of ever dimming light, and shook his head in disbelief at what his friend was doing.

Brian had timed to trip to take advantage of slack water, when the tides were at their weakest, the usual poor visibility was only made worse by the silt particles illuminating in the beam of his torch. The cold was jarring through his dry suit as he dropped down, the slick buoy line his only guidance in the ill-lit murk. With no method of depth perception, he was monitoring his head. Apart from the usual clearing of the pressure built up in the sinuses, his shoulders were tense but there was no tightness or pressure building behind his eyes at that point. He had the two extra cylinders attached to his abdomen: one for filling the lift-bags and the other to lengthen his time at the bottom and the staggered ascent. He reached the floor of The Channel after a slow two minutes and felt none the worse for it, as the cod and whiting kept darting through his shaft of light.

On not much more than a hunch, the mound in the centre rear of the site was his target, until then only serving as a feature to orientate around the wreck. From his records, he knew it had been measured at five metres long and three across at its widest point. He began jabbing one of the rods through the surface of the entire mound. Each time he struck something solid, he would excavate down through a century's coverage of silt and mud. He dug three shallow holes, at the base of each he found a chalky rock and on each occasion repeated the word "baastard" to himself. After thirty minutes the first tank was running low as he started digging a fourth hole, this time he found a flat surface at the bottom, a heavily rusted one. Further jabs with his rod gave him the rough dimensions and started digging away at either side of the object. He couldn't see what it was before the stirred sediment cleared, so collected information by running his hands over it. It felt like a safe, it was the right size and the lipped top and four feet convinced him further. The surface he originally unearthed felt very brittle and corroded. His metal rods were strong enough to break through the wafer-like metal sheeting. Through a jagged opening just large enough to fit his hand, he felt inside. Unless he was mistaken, he was feeling the ridges in between stacked ingots of some kind. His rod bounced off them as well, which made them non-ferrous ingots in a rusted safe. At the very least, they must have been silver. Copper or brass hadn't been prized enough to store in a safe. Both airbags were attached around the safe and half inflated to exert a controlled pull upwards while Brian worked at clearing the mud around the safe, adhering it to the ground. He jabbed and dragged and scored and twisted his rod through the retaining mud.

He felt a gap grow underneath the safe as the lift-bags began to fulfill their function, so Brian fully inflated them and stepped back as they started to move the safe up to the surface. Most likely they would scare the living daylights of out Bill in the process. Brian switched to his second scuba tank with his left arm hooked around the buoy line and before beginning to kick his flippers to follow the safe, he looked upwards. Awaiting Brian on the surface hung a safe half full of silver, an impending marriage to Anne and a likely buy-in on the Titanic job. All he had to do was surface, his last experience of decompression had not gone so swimmingly. With his eyes closed so he could monitor himself more closely, he let his left hand move slowly up the buoy line.

SALVAMAR – A TALE OF SALVAGE & DEEP DIVING

After Brian bobbed up and after sighting the first pulse from the lighthouse through his helmet, he muttered to himself.

"Magic!"

Author's Note

Growing up with Brian as my uncle normalised living abroad for me. Maybe it's the reason I've spent most of my adult life outside of the UK. In some ways, we were cut from similar cloth, and we always maintained contact by various means when on other sides of the globe. He was forever supportive of his most kindred of nephews and always offered the benefit of his enormous life experience. I admit, some comparisons are now undeniable.

After he passed away in December 2016, the more my interest in his life grew, the greater my understanding became. As I met more people he knew and visited more places he lived, the idea for this book grew slowly until it became inevitable/unavoidable. So much so that it was impossible to fit him all in. Thankfully, some of the details couldn't be printed (those provided by Frank Lee in the main!). I have sifted through everything that was left behind; dive log books, letters, medical reports, photos, dive records and decompression charts, divorce papers, postcards, cine films and wreck survey documents. I have also visited Athens and Marseille (twice).

Obviously parts of the dialogue, timings and incident details have had to be fictionalised to fit the plot. I've attempted to capture the spirit of the man and the way he lived, and estimate that 95% of this account is true: while the remaining 5% is as close to the truth as possible. Focusing on the period between 1970 and 1984, it avoids the latter stages of his life, where he exchanged a Maserati for a mobility scooter. And although undeniably difficult as all his family noted, he faced his illness with characteristic bravery and understatedness.

For example, I haven't included his attempt at starting an airline in 1988. Swann Air was to operate out of Stansted Airport, on far-eastern routes, and with planes that would complete with on-board casinos. Or the opening chapters of an adventure novel he wrote, involving the recovery of the mythical peacock throne, reputedly sunk on the wreck of the *Grosvenor* in South Africa and the secret salvage attempts by the Chinese Government in recovering the prized Peking Man skull from the *Awa Maru* wreck, sunk during WWII.

I tried to use as much of the material that was so kindly provided by his former colleagues, friends and loved ones as I could. I've endeavoured to use lines from his letters in speech quotes. I've emptied an entire writing pad in note-taking, a favourite pen has sadly run dry and internet search engines are well and truly fed up with me.

For someone who was absent so often, he must have had something special about him to become such an iconic figure in our clan. As every family member will concur, we miss his dry humour and terribly naughty smile. But we're mindful it was a privilege to have such a character in our special family, if for too short a time possibly.

He was a brother, a son and nearly a father on a couple of occasions. But to his nieces and nephews, he was always and will forever remain our very own 'James Bond Uncle!'

Rest in peace, Brian.

(I know you will be)

SALVAMAR – A TALE OF SALVAGE & DEEP DIVING

SALVAMAR – A TALE OF SALVAGE & DEEP DIVING

SALVAMAR

A TALE OF SALVAGE & DEEP DIVING

If you have enjoyed my uncle's many adventures, please be kind enough to leave a review. As Brian would say himself, "That would be magic!"

Contact:
Salvamarbook@gmail.com